Spring Tide

Chris Beckett is a former university lecturer and social worker living in Cambridge. He is the winner of the Edge Hill Short Fiction Award, 2009, for *The Turing Test*, the prestigious Arthur C. Clarke Award, 2013, for *Dark Eden* and was shortlisted for the British Science Fiction Association Novel of the Year Award for *Mother of Eden* in 2015 and for *Daughter of Eden* in 2016.

Also by Chris Beckett

The Holy Machine
Marcher
Dark Eden
Mother of Eden
Daughter of Eden
The Turing Test
The Peacock Cloak

Spring Tide
Chris Beckett

First published in hardback in Great Britain in 2017 by
Corvus, an imprint of Atlantic Books Ltd.

10 9 8 7 6 5 4 3 2 1

A CIP catalogue record for this book is available
from the British Library.

Hardback ISBN: 978 1 78 649 0506
E-book ISBN: 978 1 78 649 0513

Printed in Great Britain by TJ International, Ltd, Padstow

Corvus
An imprint of Atlantic Books Ltd
Ormond House
26–27 Boswell Street
London WC1N 3JZ

www.corvus-books.co.uk

For Maggie

Contents

Cellar

I've never told anyone about my cellar because I know that, as soon as I speak of it, it will cease to be truly mine. Even if issues of legal ownership were not to arise – and I'm fairly certain they would – people would want to see it, look into its origins, make it into news. I mean, good God, a thing like this could go viral, all round the world. And, even supposing that sort of media attention could in some way be avoided, my friends would certainly expect to share my find. I can imagine them now, whooping with excitement as they run up and down the stairs and along the corridors. I can almost hear them planning the parties we would have.

But that of course would be the end of everything that I most value about my cellar. If I were ever to share its secret, it would just be another bunch of rooms from that day on, however unique its construction, however mysterious its origins, however stupendous its scale. And, like so many millions of other rooms in every city and town, and in every single country all around the world, it would be given functions – storage, office space, accommodation – and be cluttered up, as other rooms are, with chairs and pictures and computers and desks and cupboards and beds and people and chitchat and TV and all the other props and rituals of that dreary and repetitive little dance that people call life. If I keep the secret, on the other hand, my cellar is something else entirely, barely of this world at all.

So I speak to no one about it, and have permanently abandoned any thought of moving anywhere else, or of embarking on any relationship which might, at some point, raise an expectation of staying over or – heaven forbid! – moving in. Not that I've had any interest in such relationships lately. At the beginning, before I'd completely absorbed the full implications of my discovery, I did still go out and meet with other people. I occasionally even invited friends back, getting a bit of a thrill, if I'm honest, from watching them in my little home, chatting and laughing about nothing as people do, without the slightest inkling of the vast and mysterious spaces beneath them. In fact, I used to give them tours of the house, the way you do, showing what I'd done with the various rooms – the knocked-through wall here, the clever little storage units there – just so I could listen to them coo about how spacious it was, how clever I was at making space. I had a job not to laugh out loud.

But as time went on, I became less interested in human interaction. Increasingly, when social opportunities were offered me, I turned them down and chose the cellar instead, until eventually the invitations all but died away. At one point I contemplated putting it about that I'd joined one of those secretive cults whose rules forbid fraternising with non-believers, and whose beliefs are sufficiently obnoxious to prevent anyone wanting to fraternise anyway. I thought it might be a way of putting an end to the last annoying trickle of invitations, as well as potentially embarrassing spur-of-the-moment visits. But these problems seem pretty much to have solved themselves now, leaving only the occasional irritant of telephone enquiries about my well-being from my more persistent friends.

When I bought the house, there had been no cellar mentioned in the details I received from the estate agent, and I'm quite sure the previous owner had no inkling of its existence. I myself found it purely by accident one day when I was investigating some loose boards in the middle of my living room floor.

Ever since I'd moved in, I'd been irritated by a patch of carpet there that subsided slightly when I stepped on it. However, when it actually came to doing something about it, the annoyance those boards caused me had always seemed pretty trivial in comparison to the time and trouble that would be involved in moving the furniture and rolling back the fitted carpet. In particular, I was put off by the prospect of shifting a largish dresser which I hadn't bothered to move even when I redecorated the room. But that particular Saturday I noticed that the wobbly board or boards had now actually stretched the carpet to the point that it never quite lay flat. Since I happened to have nothing else in particular to do that day, I decided I'd try and fix the problem right there and then.

I piled all the furniture, other than the dresser, at one end of the room. I took the drawers out of the dresser and stacked them in the hallway, and then I went next door to ask my neighbour Dave if he would help me shift the dresser itself. I had to offer Dave a cup of tea after that, of course, which was tiresome, and listen to him discuss the merits of the five interestingly different combinations of motorways and A-roads that he'd used over the years when visiting his in-laws in Doncaster. But when he'd finally gone – it was about 11 in the morning by then – I rolled back the carpet, identified the loose boards, and pulled them up to see what was going on. It turned out that one of the joists beneath them had at some point split, with the result that it was sagging slightly in the middle, and was only held together by a couple of fibres.

All that was really needed was a little extra support at the weak point, and, since the joist was only half a metre above the concrete base of the house, that was a simple matter: it could simply be propped up with bricks. To make things even easier, I happened to have some bricks in my back garden, left over from building a wall, which would be more than enough for the job. I was about to go and fetch some of them when I noticed – and I could so easily have missed it! – what looked like the corner of a metal hatch in the concrete. That was unexpected. A hatch to gain access to *where*? I pulled up more boards to allow me to get down next to it and pull it open. Inside I found a set of descending stairs, disappearing into darkness.

I felt rather excited. It seemed I had a cellar down there which had somehow been forgotten about along the way as the house passed from owner to owner. I realised that it would almost certainly be too damp to be of use – otherwise why would the stairs have been boarded over in the first place? – and, since I had the whole house to myself, I had no real need for extra room in any case. But there was something profoundly satisfying all the same about the idea of having more space at my disposal than I'd known about. I'd always hated clutter – that was the simple explanation for the spaciousness which my friends had always admired – and I'd always considered myself to be the polar opposite of a hoarder. The house was sparsely furnished, I didn't collect ornaments or keep books that I'd already read, and anything I didn't actually use any more was promptly dispatched to the dump or a charity shop. But space I liked – you could never have enough of that – and my favourite dreams were about discovering new and unexpected rooms.

Intrigued and excited as I was, though, I did hesitate before going down the stairs. I can even remember wondering whether to go round and fetch Dave again so as to have someone with me. How I've changed! It seems extraordinary to me now that I could have contemplated such a thing even for a moment! But I saw things differently then and, apart from anything else, there was a vague apprehension in the back of my mind that there might be some criminal explanation for the hidden cellar. What if there were bodies down there, for instance?

After a few seconds thought, however, I decided that Dave was unnecessary and I fetched a torch and began to descend the stairs on my own. Dead bodies would certainly not be pleasant, but they did seem rather far-fetched. And if there *were* new rooms for me at the bottom of those stairs, I wanted a chance to savour them without dreary old Dave beside me to spoil the moment by prattling on about the various cellars he'd encountered over the years, or the relative merits of plastic membranes and waterproof rendering as a means of keeping out the damp. How different everything would have turned out if I hadn't made that choice!

When I reached what I'd assumed to be the bottom of the stairs, I discovered to my surprise that I was still surrounded by concrete walls. It was simply a landing, and the stairs just turned and continued downwards. Even more strangely, the same thing happened another storey down: I reached a second landing, and there was still nowhere else to go but either down or back up again. Clearly this was no ordinary cellar. I must admit I began to feel rather scared, although it would have been difficult to say exactly why.

Three storeys down, further below the ground than the roof of my house was above it, things changed. I could *hear* the absence around me straight away and, when I pointed my torch outwards, a whole corridor revealed itself in front of me, with doors down either side. How long the corridor was I couldn't tell at that point, but it clearly extended beyond the boundary of my house, and was too long for the beam of my small torch to reach the end of it. Sweeping the beam around me, I soon discovered that it wasn't the only one. There were actually four corridors radiating out from the stairway at right angles to one another. I noticed a light switch in the corridor in front of me, and, not really expecting it to work, I flipped it on. To a distance of some fifty metres, the corridor was suddenly as bright as any normal well-lit room. There were blue doors down each side of it, five metres apart, and after every second door there was an opening into a side corridor. Beyond fifty metres, the lights hadn't come on, so the corridor disappeared into darkness. I soon established that the other corridors were just the same, and flipped on lights in all of them. But there was more. The staircase continued downwards, and when I shone my torch down the narrow well, I found that, as with the corridor, it continued beyond the distance that my beam could reach.

I felt *really* afraid then, a strange, pure terror, as if I was in one of those nightmares where nothing actually happens except for fear. Certainly my alarm didn't come from a sense of physical danger: there was no threat to myself that I could see. Nor did it come from a feeling that I was doing something that might get me into some kind of trouble. Why shouldn't I descend a staircase beneath my own house? No, as I say, it was a pure terror, a distillation of terror, that arose from my complete inability to make any sense at all of what I was looking at. What possible purpose might this place have? Who could have made it? How could it possibly have remained undetected up to now, and why was it underneath my house? It wasn't just having no answers to these questions that was frightening, it was the fact that I had no sense at all of where an answer might be found.

But it was too late to turn back. Even if I'd climbed straight back up those stairs at that point, rejoined the world above and nailed the floorboards firmly down, my house would have become an entirely different place. Until today it had been a straight-forward little semi in an ordinary street, with two bedrooms, a bathroom, a kitchen and a living room, but it could never go back to being that, any more than a piggybank-full of one-pound coins could ever again mean the same to a National Lottery winner. My house was a mere pimple now, a tiny out-crop, a shoebox made of bricks, perched above an

enormous hidden space which – such was my modest estimate at the time – quite probably had more
rooms in it than my entire street.

I was terrified and disorientated, but, even then,
I sensed the possibilities. Even at that early stage,
scared as I was, I had an inkling that what I was now
experiencing as fear might quite readily and easily be
repackaged as an intense, almost sexual, excitement.

I went to the first door on the right and, feeling
rather foolish, knocked on it. There was of course
no answer, but I found this in itself unnerving – it's
interesting, when you think about it, how ready we
are to reinterpret simple absence as sinister brood-
ing presence – and I stood in front of it for a full
minute before I'd gathered the courage to turn the
handle. The room was completely empty. I flicked
on the light switch inside the door and found the
walls pristine and white, the floor covered in a plain
grey lino that looked as if no one had ever stepped
on it. There was no furniture, no trace of human
occupation, but this one room was bigger than the
living room in the little house three storeys above
me that I supposed was still up there, although it
already seemed almost irrelevant to my life.

I stayed down there for seventeen hours in the
end, without food or drink, wandering from corridor to corridor, room to room, and descending at
least eight storeys below the ground without any
sense that I was getting near the bottom. I became

utterly enchanted, so immersed in the experience that I simply couldn't bear to interrupt or dilute it by returning even for a short while to the ordinary little world outside. When I could no longer ignore my aching bladder, I simply pissed in the corners of rooms, making a mental note to bring down a bucket and mop.

The rooms were arranged in blocks of four surrounded by corridors, and each room was exactly the same, with white walls and grey floors. Each time I opened a door I felt a frisson of anticipation and fear, wondering whether this time there'd be something there to see. Even a piece of furniture would have been a shock, or a different colour paint, let alone a human being, another mind, sitting there quietly, waiting. But I found nothing to disturb the pristine uniformity.

I think in fact that the very absence of anything new was the thing that kept me going so long, flicking on light after light after light, opening door after door. It was maddening to think there might possibly be a room I'd not yet seen that was different from the others, but at the same time, it was actually very soothing to be finding nothing at all, to be encountering, over and over again, the same calm vacancy, the same pure space, like unused graph paper uncluttered by pencilled lines or curves. The rhythm of that, the monotony of it, even almost its tediousness, was strangely compelling, like popping bubblewrap, or playing a fruit machine, or reading a newspaper you've already read many times from one end to the other. And I think it made manageable what would otherwise have been simply too much for me to contain.

It wasn't until 4 in the morning that I finally emerged, exhausted, dizzy with hunger, and parched with thirst. How poky my little living room seemed, with the furniture piled up at one end of it, and my own ghostly reflection looking back at me from the window whose curtains were still drawn back from the morning. How dreary and ordinary that street-lamp looked across the road, those parked cars, that hedge, that brass letterbox glinting meaninglessly in the electric light. I quickly snatched the curtains closed, then gobbled some tuna straight from the tin, with three ungarnished pieces of white bread and a warm bottle of beer.

I lay down on my bed after that, but I was far too agitated to be able to settle properly into sleep and, even in the short periods when I briefly nodded off, my dreams were simply a continuation of my waking experience. I was still opening doors, one after another, I was still looking into rooms. And then I'd wake and realise that it really was down there, the cellar, the corridors, the empty rooms. Several times I was on the point of abandoning the idea of rest and heading back underground, but I held myself back and, about the time that daylight first began to seep in round my curtains, I finally succumbed to exhausted sleep.

I was woken at 9.30 by my neighbour Dave pounding on my front door.

'Are you alright there, mate?'

I blinked at him. He didn't seem to notice he'd woken me. 'Yes, I'm fine.'

'Only you went all quiet yesterday. I could see the hole in the floor through your window, but you didn't seem to be there.'

'I popped out to see my mum.'

'Oh.' He stood with his mouth open for a while, staring at my face. My lie had completely floored him. 'It's just that your car was still parked on the street, and I could see your bike round the side.'

As Dave knew, my mother couldn't drive, and she lived in a village twenty-five miles away that was ten miles from the nearest station. In fact, he'd once very obligingly given me a lift there, when my car was temporarily off the road. But I reminded myself that there wasn't a law that obliged us to explain our travel arrangements to our next door neighbours.

'I said to Betty perhaps I should break down the door,' Dave went on after a difficult three-second pause which my explanation was supposed to have filled. 'Or call the police. I was really worried about you, mate. Specially when it got dark and your curtains were still wide open. I wondered whether you'd had a fall or something. I was pretty relieved when Betty got up this morning and saw your curtains drawn. "Well, they couldn't have drawn themselves, could they?" Betty said. "*So someone's* alive in there, for sure."'

'I appreciate your concern, Dave, but I'm absolutely fine.'

Fine wasn't a very accurate description of how I felt, though. I was terribly tired, and desperately agitated. What was more, though Dave had always got on my nerves, I was experiencing for the first time a whole new level of irritation that was still novel to me but was soon to become the norm in all my dealings with the outside world. As long as I was with him, I was acutely aware that every single minute the conversation lasted was a minute lost forever when I could have been under the ground, exploring the pristine spaces beneath my house.

When I'd finally managed to wrap things up with Dave, I shut the door so quickly after him that it was really more of a slam, hurried back to my living room, and was already descending the stairs when I suddenly remembered that I had friends coming for lunch.

Cursing, I climbed back out again, found my phone and called to tell them I wasn't well.

'Oh, poor Jeremy,' exclaimed my friend Liz. 'Hope you feel better soon. Anything we can do for you? Shopping or anything?'

Again, I felt that irritation. Why was she wasting my time with these trivia, when the cellar was down there waiting?

'I'll be fine, thanks,' I said and hung up, so keen to finish the call that I didn't even take the time to say goodbye.

I was hurrying back towards the cellar, when it occurred to me that I couldn't just leave things like this in my living room. Anyone who came to the house would immediately see the piled furniture, the rolled carpet, the big hole in the floor, and the descending stairs.

Seething with resentment at the wasted time, I drove to a builder's merchant at a dangerous and illegal speed, bought wood, hinges and a new rug, and hurtled back again, shooting two red lights, and getting honked at angrily by other motorists. Flinging my purchases down in my hallway, I returned to the living room and moved the furniture again so I could roll up the fitted carpet and remove it altogether. My impatience seemed to give me super-human strength and I not only shifted the dresser on my own this time, but managed to lift it right over the rolled carpet.

That done, I set to work fashioning a hinged door in the middle of my floor, which I could conceal under the new rug in case of visitors, but uncover quickly when I was alone, so as to cut delay to an absolute minimum. Through all of this I kept the curtains drawn, in spite of the sunshine outside, and in spite of the curiosity which this would in-evitably arouse in Dave. God damn it, it was none of his business! I'd always hated the benign, cow-like curiosity of Dave and my other neighbours up and down the street, beaming over their garden fences as they waited to be told the identity of a weekend visitor, the reason for an unusually early departure for work or the contents of a package they'd kindly taken in for me, but up to now I'd always felt obliged to indulge it. Not any longer, I decided. There was no time.

I'm no carpenter, and I'd forbidden myself peeks until the job was properly finished, so it was after 5 p.m. when I finally descended again into my cellar. I had an aching back and several small cuts and bruises from my furious hammering and sawing, but none of that mattered. As I put my foot on the stairs, I was in a kind of trance of anticipation at the prospect of all that space, trembling, dazed and almost floating, like an adolescent boy on the way to his very first sexual experience.

I've moved a few things down there over the months since then, and made a few changes. One of the rooms on the top level is now a store. I've left a few strategic buckets here and there: the last thing I want when I'm ten storeys or more below the world is to have to come up to the surface to take a leak. And, in a room on the twelfth level, near to the stairs, I've also established a kind of base camp, with a comfortable chair, a couch, bottled water and canned food. I can sit down there for hours quite happily, doing nothing at all other than savouring the empty, private space that I know is all around me, and listening to the extraordinary silence.

But I continue to explore as well. Lately, I've taken to sticking a blank post-it note on every door I enter, so that I'll know for certain when I've seen them all. I've never yet found a room that was different in any way from any of the others – there's never been the slightest trace of any previous occupant, or even the smallest clue as to the purpose for which all this was hollowed out – but it didn't take me very long before I found the edges. Not counting those initial flights of stairs, the twenty-second floor down is the bottom, and, on every level, each of the four radial corridors ends in a T-junction after thirty-five rooms. So each floor, in other words, is a grid that is seventy rooms deep and seventy rooms wide, and, since there are twenty-two floors, that means that my house has in excess of a hundred thousand rooms: six of them above ground and the rest below. I'd once gloated over the idea that I had as many rooms as all the rest of the street put together, but that turned out to be a ridiculous underestimate. A few corridors on a single level could equal my street. In the cellar as a whole there were as many rooms as there were people in the entire city above me. Who could blame me for not wanting to go out any more, when I have so much space of my own at my disposal?

And yet I have to admit that lately I've started to feel that it isn't quite enough. I still love my cellar, and I still appreciate its extent. But the limits are chafing a little. Without my having made a clear decision to do so, I've found myself beginning to tap on the outer walls of the perimeter corridors, listening out for the hollow sound of yet more rooms beyond the ones I've come to know. And then, of course, there's the possibility to consider of even more space *below*. Well, why not? If *this* is possible, then so is that.

Outside in the world under the sky, my old friends laugh and quarrel, meet and part, have babies, go to work, take their dogs for walks in the park, watch TV and go to the pub. Deep down below them, I am pulling up the lino on the bottom floor, searching for hatches that might take me through to new and untouched spaces.

The End of Time

Eli waited. Behind and above him was complete darkness. In front of him was an empty arena. His fellow archangels around its perimeter were shadowy forms in the dimness, waiting silently, just as he was doing himself, for the performance to begin.

A single tall figure stepped forward into the middle. From the pitch darkness beyond the arena, a great sigh arose from countless unseen watchers, spreading outwards and upwards like a tide. For this new presence was no mere archangel, this was the Clockmaker himself. He stood out there for a moment, while silence fell once more, and then he raised his hand. *Pouf!* – a brilliant point of light appeared, suspended above them all.

Again that great sigh came from the darkness on every side and, in the intense brightness of that tiny light, Eli glimpsed for a moment the cherubim and seraphim out there, the dominions and thrones. Tier after tier, this whole vast angelic host had been waiting for all eternity to admire the Clockmaker's work.

The point of light expanded rapidly, diminishing in brightness as it did so, until almost the whole arena was filled by a huge dim sphere, leaving just sufficient space round the edge for the archangels to keep their vigil. It was time for Eli and his companions to get to work, and they set to it at once, each one leaning forward to peer intently into the depths of the sphere.

Straight away, Eli saw lights in there. He saw great skeins of light, strewn through the void, each one made up of millions of little disc-shaped clumps of glowing matter that span around like wheels. And when Eli examined the wheels closely, he found that they too were made of smaller parts. They were tenuous structures of the most extraordinary delicacy, consisting almost entirely of empty space. These wheel-shapes were not solid clumps as they had at first appeared, but were so full of emptiness as to be almost imaginary: wheels sketched out in the darkness by billions of separate specks of light, each one following its own allotted path. And Eli saw that, as these little specks travelled round and round the centre of each wheel, waves of pressure passed through them, so that the specks clumped closer together when the wave reached them, and moved apart again as it passed by, creating graceful spiral bands of brightness that themselves moved round the wheel. Each tiny wheel was really two wheels revolving at different speeds: a wheel of specks, and a wheel of waves that moved through the specks!

Laughing with delight, Eli turned from the spectacle to point it out to the hidden watchers who were seated, row after row, on the dark tiers behind him. 'Observe!' he cried. 'The same matter forms two separate wheels simultaneously!'

A sigh of appreciation rose up among the cherubim and seraphim, the thrones and dominions. But, even before the sigh had faded, another archangel on the far side of the arena was calling out just as excitedly as Eli had done: 'Look! Even the smallest of these lights has tiny spheres revolving round it!'

Again the sigh in the darkness.

'Notice how they also spin on their own axes!' called a third archangel.

Another sigh.

'And see how the whole spreads outwards!' called a fourth. 'This whole area is constantly expanding, just so as to be able to contain it.'

The Clockmaker had created Time, no less, and here in front of them, wheel within wheel, was the Great Clock that gave it form.

Sigh after sigh rolled outwards and upwards in the darkness.

Gradually the initial excitement subsided. The archangels called out only rarely now, and those awed sighs, rising in one part or another of the vast and unseen auditorium, happened less and less frequently. So rare had they become, in fact, that many aeons had passed in complete silence when the archangel Gabriel suddenly spoke.

He had been giving his attention to the smallest

elements of the Clock, and had focused his vision to such an extent that he could see not only the tiny motes of stone that revolved round each star, but the surfaces of those stones, and the tiny objects that lay on those surfaces, and even the minuscule particles, wheels themselves, of which those tiny objects were made. And, on the surface of one of these stones, he had made an strange discovery.

'Observe, Clockmaker!' he said with a bow. 'A new clock has appeared within your own!'

The Clockmaker had been busy elsewhere, but, hearing this news, he looked across at once, his huge blazing eyes piercing through all the intervening nebulae and galactic clusters, to home in on the stone which Gabriel was pointing to. Eli looked too, of course. The stone was a rocky shell, still molten on the inside, of a kind so common throughout the Clock that they could be found spinning around almost every star. Minor irregularities pocked its surface. There were little bumps and hollows, and, as sometimes occurred on these half-cooled stones, liquid water had gathered in the hollows. But Gabriel was looking *into* that liquid, pointing at objects so minute that they were as small in relation to the half-cooled stone as the stone itself was small in relation to the galaxy that contained it. These new, tiny objects took the form of little spheres, moving this way and that through the water.

Now of course stars, stones, water and specks of dust were all parts of the Great Clock, and, a clock being an assemblage of moving parts, they were *meant* to move in relation to one another. But the Clockmaker could see at once that what Gabriel had found was a new *kind* of movement, and so could Eli, and the other archangels, and the hidden host. These microscopic spheres weren't simply being pushed and pulled by the forces around them. They weren't just being tugged downwards by gravity, or lifted by buoyancy, or tossed about by the convection currents that kept the water constantly turning over.

No, the motion of these little spheres was something else entirely, for it was driven from within themselves. Chemical processes unfolding inside them provided energy to thousands of tiny fibres on their outer surfaces, and these fibres were beating together in rhythmic waves that sent the little spheres rolling and tumbling through the water in directions that couldn't be explained by gravity, buoyancy or currents.

Along with all the other archangels, Eli could see at once that Gabriel had spoken the truth: each of these little spheres was indeed another clock in its own right. But what particularly fascinated Eli was the way they perpetuated themselves. They weren't bodies of matter in the way that a star or a planet or a stone was a body of matter. Rather they were patterns that passed *through* matter, just as those spiral pressure waves he himself had spotted had passed through drifts of stars, or ripples passed through water, or sounds passed through the air. In every single moment, each of those minuscule spheres was simultaneously taking in new matter from its surroundings, and expelling matter from within itself. In a very short time, each one had completely replaced the building blocks of which it was made. And yet, like a spiral arm, it still retained the same essential form.

And what a form! There was silence in the arena and in the darkness beyond, and the archangels glanced uneasily at one another. They all knew that the Clockmaker hadn't built these tiny structures, that they had arisen on their own, and were a purely accidental by-product of the forces that the Clockmaker had set in motion, much as the complicated eddies and cross-currents of a mountain stream are a by-product of its headlong rush downhill. And yet, accidental or not, there was an obvious fact in front of them which they could all see but none of them dared name out loud: every one of these little rolling spheres was at least as complex and as perfect as the Great Clock in its entirety. What would their master think about that?

The Clockmaker frowned. He was omniscient, of course, so he was far ahead of all the rest of them, and he'd seen at first glance what his angels and archangels had only gradually grasped. Each of those little rolling spheres, he could see, wasn't simply *as* intricate as his own Clock, but far far more so. Indeed, considered in terms of complexity, his Clock was as tiny in relation to these little spheres, as they were to it in terms of size. And, as if that wasn't bad enough, the Clockmaker had noticed something else as well that none of the archangels had yet spotted: these things were changing over time. At any given moment, hundreds of thousands of them were splitting themselves in two, and the smaller spheres resulting from the division would then immediately begin to take in matter from the rich solution around them, growing quickly to full size again, and then themselves dividing. Naturally, small errors occurred at each new division. These were usually negligible in their effects, but occasionally they resulted in clocks that were too badly flawed to be able to maintain their separateness from the surrounding matter, so that they simply broke down and disappeared. What the Clockmaker had noticed, though, was that, in an absolutely infinitesimal proportion of cases, the new clocks actually proved to be *superior* to their precursors, in the sense that they were even more finely attuned to the task of maintaining their own integrity against the forces of entropy all around them. And therefore, because the types of clock that were most successful at retaining their separateness were the ones that increased in numbers, the design of these little clocks in general (if the word 'design' could be used in such a context) was constantly increasing in sophistication.

With his divine foresight, which was really a capacity to see not just in three dimensions but in four, five and even six, the Clockmaker looked ahead through time with his great fiery eyes. He observed the trajectory of development of these tiny intricate clocks, and saw them diversifying and spreading, like a kind of restless rust that would gradually form itself again and again from the simple minerals of which a planet was made, until that planet's entire surface was covered with a multiplicity of wriggling, bulging, blooming forms, climbing over one another, consuming one another, driving one another to yet higher levels of adaptation and complexity. Ultimately, he saw, this would affect the mechanism of the Great Clock itself in small but subtle ways. It would change the albedo of planetary surfaces, for instance, and in so doing, minutely alter the workings of the entire design.

'Wipe it clean!' he commanded.

Gabriel, that great archangel, bowed his head in submission, and reached with his hand deep into the Clock until his fingers were almost touching that little, spinning, half-cooled rock. He frowned with concentration for a moment as cleansing rays came pouring out from his fingertips, scorching the surface of the little stone, annihilating the tiny spheres and all their kin, and breaking down all but the most rudimentary of chemical bonds, so that the stone was returned in a matter of moments to its previous state as a simple mechanical component of the Clock.

A sigh rose and spread, outwards and upwards, through the multitude in the darkness beyond the arena. And Eli watched in silence from his own quiet corner.

'Listen! All of you!' the Clockmaker boomed out to his archangels. 'Note carefully what Gabriel has just done and do exactly the same! That is a command, to be followed without exception. You must watch your sectors constantly for any unscheduled developments of that kind, and, as soon as you find them, they must be wiped away at once. Nothing must be allowed to tarnish my Clock's perfection, or to disturb the smooth, clean flow of Time.'

So from then on each archangel carefully audited every one of the billions of planets within his area of control for the first signs of that strange new restless rust. And from time to time, only occasionally at first but gradually more frequently, one or other of them would suddenly reach into the Clock and blast clean the surface of some small stone that had showed signs of developing patterns on its surface that might possibly be able to replicate themselves.

Each time, the invisible host would sigh.

Like all the others, Eli watched his own little section of the Clock – his own galaxies, his own stars, his own planets – and for a long time, he did just as Gabriel had done and as the other archangels were now doing. Again and again, he reached in with his hand to wipe away imperfection with blasts of purifying energy.

He had done this many thousands of times when he spotted yet another stone on which a film of organic matter was starting to grow. Following his now-familiar routine, he extended his hand into the Clock in a business-like fashion and was about to let loose the cleansing rays when, for some reason, he hesitated. All the other archangels round him were still blasting away – there was Raphael for instance, over to his left, shooting out deadly rays right at that very moment – but Eli found, to his own surprise, that this time he simply couldn't bring himself to do it. In fact, far from reaching in to destroy this new collection of little self-replicating clocks, he found himself shielding them so they couldn't be seen by anyone other than himself. And, having done that, he amazed himself further by abandoning his vigil over the millions of other planets in his sector and instead settling down to watch the tiny clocks he'd saved as they very slowly grew and changed.

Time went by. That little stone wheeled around its star many hundreds of millions of times while Eli watched the little clocks on its surface. And he became so rapt, so enchanted, so focused on this one single stone, that he didn't even notice the huge fiery eyes of the Clockmaker turning in his direction, homing in on him alone through all the spinning wheels of the Clock, and recognising at once what he was doing.

'Eli, my son,' the Clockmaker boomed. 'You have disobeyed me.'

Eli started, rigid with terror, while gasps of shock echoed and re-echoed through the vast auditorium around them.

'I *have* disobeyed you, Father,' Eli acknowledged. He fell to his knees as the Clockmaker came striding through his own creation to stand towering above his disobedient servant. 'And now, I know, it's for you to decide what you wish to do with me.'

The Clockmaker shrugged. 'Just wipe it clean, Eli,' he said, with the merest of glances at the tiny world Eli had been watching for all those millions of years. 'Wipe it clean, and, just this once, we'll say no more about it.'

It was not so much a sigh this time as a gasp that arose around them in the darkness. Eli had been extraordinarily lucky – archangels had been exiled or annihilated for much smaller acts of dis-obedience – but, instead of gratefully accepting the lifeline, he stubbornly stood his ground.

'I won't, Father,' he said. 'I want to leave it alone, and see how it develops.'

Once again, like the sound of some great unseen ocean moving restlessly in its bowl, a sigh rippled back and up through the auditorium, to be followed by a deep expectant silence, as if the entire host was holding its breath.

Surprised by his servant's intransigence, the Clockmaker looked back with slightly more interest at the growth on the surface of the little planet. Why did this matter so much to Eli, he was asking himself?

With his omniscience and foreknowledge, he could see not only how Eli's little clocks were functioning in the present, but how they would develop between now and the end of time if allowed to continue on their present trajectory. And he quickly established that, in this particular case, the effect on the Great Clock would be negligible, for it so happened that this small planet, and its star, and even the galaxy of which they formed a part, were relatively peripheral parts of the grand design.

'Master,' Eli persisted, 'those tiny beings there, those little clocks, have developed in a strange new way that goes far beyond anything we've seen before. They've become a different thing entirely from those spheres that Gabriel found. In fact, some of them have become almost as *we* are. For they *see*, Father, they know they exist, and they are aware of the Clock moving around them as something separate to themselves. They've even begun to wonder what the Great Clock is, and who made it, and what purpose it serves.'

He didn't *really* speak in words of course, and nor did the Clockmaker when he answered, for words would have been utterly inadequate to the speed and power of their thought. Rather, in each instant, the two of them laid out whole philosophies, entire sequences of thought, complete with every possible ramification, permutation and implication. It was as if, in each exchange, an entire new science was invented, developed and brought to completion.

So it always was between the Clockmaker and his archangels.

Again the Clockmaker shrugged as he half-watched the countless varieties of tiny clock on the surface of that little stone, his interest already fading.

'They *are* like us in some respects,' he conceded. 'But look how they must suffer to be so.'

Suffering was outside Eli's experience, and the Clockmaker's too, but the Clockmaker spoke of it by way of practical demonstration. He showed Eli pain, fear, grief and horror, first of all as they appeared from outside, and then as they were experienced from within, laying out millions of beautifully categorised examples. And he demonstrated with irrefutable logic that these various unpleasantnesses were the inevitable lot of these tiny beings.

'These entities only exist at all because of suffering.' That, very roughly speaking, was the gist of the Clockmaker's argument. 'They only continue to exist because their mechanisms drive them to constantly struggle against annihilation. They are fragile teetering towers. If they are not just to crumble and melt back into the world, everything that threatens their precarious balance must be the cause of fear and pain to them, while everything likely to maintain and perpetuate it must be the source of craving, the cause of constant striving and desperate struggle. There can never be rest for them, for as soon as they rest they will topple, and disintegrate, and cease to exist.'

And Clockmaker laid out more examples. There

was a man trapped inside a sinking ship, trying
to suck air from the dwindling pocket that still
remained, a woman surrounded by a forest fire,
vainly trying to shield her children from the blaze
with her own blistering flesh. All that was really
going to happen to the woman and her children was
that their bodies would oxidise, and then quickly
return to the peaceful simplicity of the untarnished
Clock. All that would happen to the drowning man
was that his own personal clock would stop. Yet still
they struggled desperately, even when all hope had
gone of retaining their separateness.

'Don't you pity them, Eli?' the Clockmaker asked.
'Don't you pity these strange accidental beings, which
are neither one thing nor another? They *are* like us
in a way – you're quite right about that – they're like
angels, and that is indeed a strange thing. But can't
you see they're angels made of mud, who must constantly worry about rain, and fret about heat, if they
are to remain in existence at all? Surely it would be
better to take away from them this cruel desperate
battle that they are compelled to fight, and which in
the end they'll always lose? Surely it must be better to
let them crumble quietly back down into the simple,
untroubled matter from which they come?'

'But these exist also!' protested Eli, proceeding to
lay out millions of examples, just as the Clockmaker
had done, but this time of happiness, pleasure, love,
beauty and delight, all of which, like suffering, had
hitherto been quite unknown.

If pain was real, then so were they: that was Eli's argument. But the Clockmaker just laughed.

'Alright, Eli, my stubborn son, I will give you a choice. You can destroy these little beings and come back to obedience, or you can let them survive. But if you decide to let them carry on, you yourself will have to live out, one by one, every single life that has ever existed on this stone, and exists now, and will exist in the future. Do you understand me? You must sit behind every single pair of eyes from the moment those eyes open to the moment they finally close. And then straight onto the next pair, and the next, and the next, billions and billions of times over, from now until the moment that the last eyes close.'

As the Clockmaker spoke, his own fiery eyes were drilling deep into Eli's mind. 'So come on now, Eli. Make your choice. Let's see if you really mean what you say about their lives being worth living.'

Eli looked up fearfully into the Clockmaker's terrifying gaze and saw the pure and absolute justice of what he'd said. If it was indeed true, as Eli had claimed, that these beings' existence was worth more than nothing, then how could he object to living behind their eyes?

As he tried to decide whether or not he'd really meant what he said, he turned his attention back to that little stone of his and considered once more the tiny beings who lived there. There was no doubt about it: the Clockmaker was right about suffering. These odd, accidental little beings did indeed experience terrible suffering, and it was indeed integral to their nature, essential to their continued existence. Could he really bring himself to live through it, again and again and again, until the last spark of life had finally flickered out?

Eli thought about it for a short while – the stone went round its star barely a hundred times – and then he made a decision.

'I submit to your judgement, Clockmaker. I'll let them live and I'll pay the price for it.'

The Clockmaker nodded, grudgingly impressed, and then, all at once, he dissolved Eli's angelic body, plucked out the widthless point that contained his spirit, and readied himself to fling it down to the surface of that small and insignificant stone.

'Very well then, Eli,' he boomed. 'You've made your choice. Come and look for me at the end of time.'

So Eli lived, one after the other, the lives of every sentient being born on the planet Earth. He was every human being and every animal. He was every tyrant and every slave. He was all the women who died in childbirth, and all who lived and gave birth. He was every torturer and everyone who was ever tortured. He was every beggar and every passer-by, every cat and every mouse, every hawk and every sparrow. He looked out at the world through the multiple eyes of all the spiders that ever were, the compound eyes of every ant and fly, the lidless eyes of every fish. He experienced the abyssal depths through the senses of each blind creature that wriggled or crawled there. He was every single living thing, however humble, that had some sense of its own existence, however slight that might be. And everything that any one of them experienced, he experienced himself, from the sweetest pleasure to the most excruciating pain.

After each life came to an end, he woke to himself again for a moment, saw the life he'd just lived laid out behind him, and saw the ways in which he might have lived it better. But then the moment of clarity was over, and he was back at the beginning of another life, his entire existence confined once more to a tiny memory-less bundle of flesh which must learn everything all over again. Occasionally, in certain human bodies, some vague sense of his situation would come to him, and he'd try to communicate it to his fellow beings. (And they, not remembering who they were, would almost always dismiss it, often angrily, and sometimes with murderous rage.) Most of the time, though, he had no inkling at all.

And so he went on. Even when all the humans had died out, he wasn't even halfway to the end of it. Millions of years passed by when he went through cockroaches, one after another, each in its dim and solitary world, with craving, pain and pleasure switching on and off in its brain like coloured lights, and no thoughts at all.

At last, though, at the end of time, when the Clock

finally stopped moving, and all its components had become cold and dark and inert, Eli returned to the place where the Clock was made. He was himself again, he was Eli the archangel, but he was immensely old. In fact, he was immeasurably older than the Clock itself, for he'd had to live out every second over and over again, through every being that had been present in it.

As he came to the place where the arena had stood, he remembered the life he'd led before his fall to Earth. He remembered what it was to be an archangel. He remembered the great fiery eyes of the Clockmaker. He remembered the sense of expectation in the darkness beyond the arena, the sighing that rose upward and outwards through that cavernous space that contained the unseen host.

But there was no sighing now, no expectation. No one spoke or moved. There wasn't even a lonely wind such as might blow through a desolate place on Earth, making things rattle and clank.

'Clockmaker!' he called out. 'It's me, Eli. I did what you asked me to do, and I've returned!'

But there was no one there. There was nothing in existence but Eli himself.

Love

'What do I love best in all the world?' Mike Staines answers himself without the slightest hesitation. 'This key fob! I've had it more than fifteen years! It's solid steel. Go on. Hold it. It's satisfying, isn't it? You can really feel the weight of it in your hand.'

There are three pint glasses on the table, each about two-thirds full.

'Fifteen years I've had it,' Mike says. 'I got it in America. Everyone thinks I've had it engraved with my initials but actually it already had MS on it when I bought it. There was a company in Pittsburgh called Maximum Steel, apparently, and it used to give these things out as gifts to customers. I bought it in a little junk shop in Philadelphia, when I lived over there in the early nineties.'

The key fob is like a slender matchbox in shape, but with rounded-off edges and corners. Set into one face of it is a tiny sphere which Mike rolls back and forth with his thumb, showing on one side a black MS enamelled on a white background, and on the other, a white MS on black.

'Look at that woman over there with the purple

scarf,' says Dave Greaves. 'Look at her with her nice new haircut trying to *be* someone. Here I am, she's saying, I am Judy Fotherington – or Kath Hessel-thwaite, or Trish Underwood or whatever her name might be – I am Judy Fotherington and this is what I stand for and this is what I am doing in the world, and this is how I choose to look.'

Mike presses a catch on the side of his key fob.

'There's a complete set of little tools in here, look, miniature versions of the stuff that Maximum Steel used to sell. They fit so snugly inside that you wouldn't know they were there. A little can opener and bottle opener. A screwdriver on the end. And scissors, look, and a metal toothpick, and here – look – a little blade. They're real tools too, even though they're so small. I've used all of them at one time or another. You know those moments when you need a bottle opener, or wish you had a knife? Well, here they are and they do the job perfectly. They just need a little drop of oil and a wipe down once in a while.'

He snaps the catch closed and the little tools are gone.

'But in every city in the land,' says Dave, 'there are thousands of women like Judy Fotherington, who stand for all the same kinds of things, are involved in all the same kinds of activities, wear the same kinds of clothes, go out with the same sort of nice but ulti-mately disappointing men as that bald bloke there she's looking so delighted with.'

Mike turns the keyfob in his hand, its cargo of keys jangling beneath it.

'I really like looking after it,' he says. 'That's the other thing about it. I polish it every week or two. That's why it looks so shiny and new.'

Apart from those pint glasses on the table, there are two packets of dry-roasted nuts and a silver tobacco tin with an ornate letter J embossed into its lid.

'It probably sounds crazy,' Mike goes on, 'but with this in my pocket I feel stronger, as if this little toolkit *equips* me somehow. Do you know what I mean? The tools and the keys equip me for life. Not that I'm superstitious, mind you. Not at all. Well, you know that, don't you? You know I don't believe in anything supernatural. Homeopathy, acupuncture, you name it: I can't be doing with any of that stuff. But that's the really great thing about my key fob. It doesn't work by magic.'

'People don't understand numbers,' Dave says. 'That's the thing. I mean, if I asked you how many people there were in this city you'd say – what? – getting on for half a million? You'd say that, and you'd think you'd answered my question, but do you really know what half a million means? I mean, just quickly, without stopping to work it out, do you think there'll be half a million days in your life? No, nothing *like*. It won't even be forty thousand. You could be introduced to ten new people every day of your life, from the day you were born to the day you die, and you still wouldn't have met the number of people who live in this city.'

'Psychology, yes,' says Mike, 'but not magic.'

'And this is just one city,' says Dave, 'and not even a particularly big one. Yet there's that woman in the purple scarf, and that bald chap with her, trying to be characters, trying to be individuals, trying to persuade themselves they signify something.'

Jeffrey Timms laughs. 'Well, perhaps they *do*, you miserable sod! What makes you so sure they don't?'

'There's just one problem with this key fob,' says Mike. 'I'm frightened I'll lose it. I know it sounds daft but I worry about it every single day. I mean I could drop it down a drain, couldn't I? Or someone could steal it. Or I could leave it behind on a train, or a bus, or in a taxi. It's nearly happened more than once, I can tell you. And the maddening thing is that there was another fob exactly the same as this one in the shop where I found it. I just wish I'd bought it while I had the chance and kept it as a spare. Believe it or not, sometimes I actually wake up in the middle of the night and lie there kicking myself that I missed the chance to have that other one sitting safely at the back of a drawer somewhere in case of need. But then I think: no, that would take away from this one. The whole charm of this is it's the only one I'll ever have. That's the point of it really.'

He sighs.

'But it *is* hard. In fact, to be honest with you, the

worry about losing it almost cancels out the pleasure of owning it at all.'

There are twelve tables in the room, each one surrounded by human beings.

'And how many pubs are there?' asks Dave. 'How many pubs in this city? Sadly not as many as there were, but I reckon it must still be about two hundred or so, wouldn't you say?'

'Sometimes I think it would be easier if I just threw it away,' says Mike Staines.

'Hard to put a figure on how many of them are *this* kind of pub,' Dave goes on, 'the kind that people like us drink in, I mean, and people like Judy Fotherington there and that bald guy, but let's say twenty per cent. I reckon it's probably more than that, but let's just say twenty. That still makes – what? – forty pubs in this one city where, on this very night, there's—'

'Or even give it to someone else,' says Mike, 'just so as to be free from the worry of it.'

Jeffrey laughs and pats him on the back.

'Well, that's love for you, mate,' he says.

The Lake

When the first clamour of birds came sweeping across the lake, the professor's wife was already wide awake. It was going to be one of those grey luminous days, she knew, when every splash and croak was full of meaning, and things suddenly happened with no apparent cause. She needed to get outside.

But the professor ate his breakfast very slowly, with the paper propped in front of him against a jar of honey.

'Good lord!' he observed amiably. 'What will this awful government do *next*!'

'Just *go*,' she answered him in her head. 'Just drink down your coffee and go!'

He spread another piece of toast, first with butter and then with marmalade, being meticulously careful in each case to go right out to the very edge of the slice. Then he poured himself a second cup, and turned the page.

'Situation in Europe looks pretty dire.' He took a bite from his toast and chewed thoughtfully while he continued to read.

What did he need to read the news for anyway?

He'd be listening to it on his radio all the way to work, the same stories over and over.

As soon as he'd gone, the professor's wife rushed out. She didn't take a picnic, or a flask, or a bottle of water. She didn't even bother with a coat. She just ran straight down to the lake. There were paths and boardwalks down there that led through the reeds, across the creeks, and between the stands of waterlogged willows. She wandered back and forth, round the bays and prominences, the little beaches, the twisted trees, the decaying wooden jetty. She was listening intently to every little sound, while all the time trying her best not to hear. She was looking everywhere for the smallest signs, but trying simultaneously not to see them. When water birds came and went from the surface, she felt the perturbations juddering right through her. And when bubbles or eddies rose from the depths, stirred up no doubt by creatures hidden below, she softly groaned as if it was her own skin that had been breached.

The sun came out and went in again. There were showers of rain, perforating the entire lake with exploding pinpricks, and her dress was soon soaked through. She barely noticed it, though, any more than she noticed her own hunger or thirst.

Early in the evening, exhausted, cold and parched, she spotted an egret standing alone on the mound of an old swan's nest. The graceful white creature was her favourite among all the inhabitants of the lake, and she clasped her hands together with delight as it tipped back its head and opened its beak as if to sing.

But no sound came. Instead, thrusting itself out from the egret's throat, came the head and neck of an old grey gander, which the graceful white bird had somehow swallowed alive.

The professor's wife groaned. Always when she wasn't expecting it! Always when, just for a moment, she'd lowered her guard!

She watched in horror as the gander stretched down with his thick coarse neck, to pull and tear and rip with his serrated beak at the delicate creature that held him prisoner. When he'd finally managed to tear himself free, all that was left of the egret was soiled white feathers and bloody flesh, with a head at one end and legs at the other.

'Ha!' honked the gander. And he turned his head sideways, as birds will do, so as to be able to stare triumphantly at the professor's wife with a single small hard eye.

The world was breaking up now. Its smooth surface had been breached, and the present and the absent, the possible and the impossible, were swapping places at will. The gander gave the professor's wife a sly wink, and then put two finger-like feathers into his beak to give a loud goosy whistle. Almost at once, four tiny white horses the size of cats came trotting along the boardwalk, harnessed to a tiny carriage. The gander reached into the carriage and took from it a red checked jacket, a yellow tie and a trilby hat. She watched him put them on, and saw him attach the bloody remains of his enemy to the back axle.

'Gee up!' the gander yelled, climbing up into the driver's seat, cracking a whip, and thundering straight at her along the boardwalk.

'If you can't get justice from others,' the gander honked as he went by, 'you just have to take it for yourself!'

The head of the egret broke away from the spine and flew spinning into the water.

'You have to look after number one in this life!' the gander squawked as he came hurtling back again, lashing his miniature horses until they bled. And off he went again round a corner, to disappear into the rushes, the egret's legs and spine bouncing along behind him.

The professor's wife ran weeping back towards her home, hoping to reach it before the gander could pass her again. But she wasn't quick enough. Even as the house was coming into view, here he was again, rumbling towards her at tremendous speed along the boards with much lashing of the whip and terrified frothing of his tiny horses' mouths.

'Attempted murder, that's what it was!' shrieked the gander, who obviously knew her fondness for the pure white bird. 'Attempted murder, no less!'

Water voles and frogs stuck their heads out of the water and stared. A furtive coot paused in mid-step to take a look, as it stalked among the reeds. And so did a hawk at the very top of a willow. The hawk was clasping a still-living swallow in its deadly claws, but paused even so to take in the scene below. And so too did the swallow: predator and prey together cocked their heads to watch the scene with identical beady eyes.

It wasn't the noisy gander going to and fro in his coach and four that they were staring at, though. They paid small heed to that silly vulgar creature, and none to the poor egret, which was now reduced to a single leg, from which hung a few torn tendons in a muddy fringe. No, it was *her* they all watched with such interest, their heads cocked this way or that the better to see: it was the professor's wife.

Sobbing, she ran through the front gate of her house, that beautiful big house that she and her husband had chosen for the way it looked out over the tranquil water. Her face wet with tears, she ran up the steps and through the door, slamming it shut behind her.

The professor worked in a city some distance away. She always imagined him there constructing a gigantic house of cards, and she visualised this painstaking activity taking place in an oak-panelled room that centuries of beeswax had saturated with its brownish honey smell, and darkened until it was almost black. The addition of two more cards, as she understood it, might take a week or even a month of planning, and the tower as it now stood was the work of several decades, yet, in her imagination at least, a moment's lapse could still bring down the whole structure in its entirety, so that total unblinking concentration was necessary for hours on end. As a result, when the professor came home, he often couldn't concentrate at all on even the simplest matters. She'd speak to him and he'd make every effort to listen, but, still engrossed with his house of cards whether he wanted to be or not, he could draw no meaning from her words.

'Is that you, darling?' he called out from the living room. 'I didn't know how long you'd be so I made us a cold supper. I left yours in the kitchen.'

As she didn't reply, he came out to see what was up. His face was mild, boyish and utterly transparent. She could see the panic rising inside him, as he took in the state of her, her sodden dress, her lank hair, her eyes red with crying. Not *again*, she could see him thinking, dear God, not this *again*.

She was a good deal younger than him, and what he had wanted from her when they married was that she be someone to *come home to*: a gentle, uncritical presence who would always just be *there*. And she'd been happy at first to play that part, or if not happy then willing. She'd greeted him with tempting little dishes she'd made, or whimsical things for the house that she'd picked up in some junk store for next to nothing. But these days, he often stayed late at work, or even slept there overnight on some pretext or another, just so as to avoid a homecoming.

'Poor darling, you are absolutely drenched,' was what he said, though. He wasn't an unkind man, and his concern was genuine, though he couldn't quite hide the dismay in his voice, or his fear about what might follow. 'First thing you need to do is get into some dry things.'

He glanced wistfully back into the living room, with its smooth cream walls, its muted lights, its expensive and understated furnishings. He saw the colourful pictures flickering and dancing across the TV screen. He heard the TV's loud and enthusiastic voice. All he wanted was to watch it all evening until the time came to sleep, thinking about nothing at all.

'The egret's been killed,' his wife announced bleakly.

She was so thin these days. She hardly ate at all.

'Oh, shame. A fox, I suppose?'

She didn't reply. He knew nothing of the coarse gander with his trilby hat, or the carriage and its tiny horses.

'I'll get changed,' she said.

'You do that, dearest. You are a silly old thing, you know! Why on Earth didn't you put on a coat?'

He glanced back hopefully at the TV.

The professor's wife snatched the curtains quickly together across her bedroom window. She wasn't quite quick enough to prevent herself from glimpsing some sort of activity going on out there beside the lake, but she refused to look, and now, whatever it was, the thick folds of fabric held it at bay. The mirror had no curtain to cover it, though, so she had to turn her back to it as she peeled off her sodden dress, for she knew that the shadow inside her was growing again, and she did *not* want to see the signs. When she'd removed her underwear, she stood for some time, naked and shivering, before she was able to summon the energy to towel herself down and pull on new clothes.

Then she went down to the kitchen. Her husband had left her some ungarnished leaves of lettuce, a tomato, some crisps and a slice of cheese. Coldly she scraped it all into the waste bucket. Then she turned on a tap and, for several minutes held the plate beneath it, letting the warm water run over her hands. After a while, the professor emerged from the living room a second time and asked if he could do anything to help. He was trying his best to find out what was troubling her, while simultaneously hoping to keep her just calm enough that he wouldn't have to find out at all.

'No,' she said flatly.

This frightened him so much that he retreated, not back to the living room this time, where she might possibly follow, but to his study, where she never came, 'to finish off some work,' as he said.

She sat down in front of the TV for a while, but she found that, just at the moment when her mind was beginning to grasp hold of an image and make some vague sort of sense of it, it was snatched away from her again and replaced with another. All she could think about was the pressure growing within her, and the dark lake outside.

'Pull yourself together!' she told herself firmly, knowing all too well where all this was leading. 'We can't always have what we want. And we can't just give way to our own impulses.'

She'd said this often enough, after all, to all those feathery ne'er-do-wells around the lake who came to her with sorry tales of their foolish, bungled lives: 'It's no good thinking we can put things right for ourselves by taking from others what isn't ours. That just makes life harder for everyone.'

And as they stood there dripping into muddy puddles, they would hang their beaks in shame, their caps pressed respectfully against their chests.

'We can't just give way to our impulses,' the professor's wife repeated to herself firmly as she lay in her bed, waiting for her husband to finish reading.

Even at four years old she had expostulated with the foolish children who spoiled things for themselves by splashing paint all over their colouring books, and not even *trying* to keep between the lines.

'It's more fun if you do things properly,' she'd told them.

All they'd be left with, after all, when they'd finished messing about, was a shapeless brown mess, and why bother with a colouring book at all if that was what you wanted? But they wouldn't listen. They just laughed at her, and carried on shouting and fooling about while she sat all by herself across the room, carefully applying the colours in their proper places, and taking great care not to cross the lines.

But, for all that, as soon as her husband had turned off his light, kissed her on the cheek, and settled into a steady rhythm of snores, the professor's wife jumped up and crept in her nightdress down to the kitchen. The fridge hummed in the warm darkness. The clock ticked on the wall. A red standby light, like a tiny glowing fire, dimly illuminated a wooden block of knives that happened to stand beside it. Her hands were shaking with excitement as she slid back the bolts on the back door and turned the key. And then there it was in front of her, with no curtains to hide it: the great black night.

'Out you go then, trouble,' she whispered to her shadow.

And she heard its throaty chuckle as it skipped off down to the lake in its little black dress and heels.

It *would* bring trouble, there could be no doubt about that, but it was still an enormous relief to let it go. Feeling almost weightless, she returned to bed, climbed in beside her still-snoring husband and sank into sleep at once.

But an hour later she was awake again.

Sounds came from the lake through the open window: croakings and patterings, plashes and reedy sighs. And behind those sounds, others, so faint as to be hardly sounds at all. Moans of pleasure, they seemed to be, or gasps, or muffled laughter.

For a long time, she lay there listening to the life beyond the walls of the house, and fighting the temptation to peer out. But finally a sudden loud splash was too much for her and she rushed to the window with a pounding heart, convinced that she would see her reckless shadow doing some awful thing like diving naked from the wooden jetty, with the whole lakeside watching, and maybe the gander in his waistcoat and his trilby hat, shouting out ribald encouragement. After all, didn't her shadow long more than anything else to feel the world against its naked skin?

But no, the jetty was empty and the water around it calm. The clouds had cleared and the lake was so smooth that it seemed not so much a body of water as a silver membrane, gossamer-thin, stretched out between two great hemispheres of stars.

'Are you alright there, darling?' her husband murmured as she returned to bed.

She didn't answer him. In fact, she hardly noticed him speak. She just lay down again and carried on listening to the night outside.

After another hour of wakefulness she jumped up again, having this time managed to convince herself that she could hear the creak and slosh of a rowing boat out on the lake, and the careless shadow singing and joking in the bow, stripped naked to the waist, while its admiring companions – the fox perhaps, and the hare with his foppish beret – laughed and cheered as they pulled together at the oars.

But there was no boat, no shadow, no fox or hare, only a single swan drifting sleepily under the moon. Paired with its perfect reflection in the still water, it resembled a scorpion, a giant scorpion of the stars crossing some vast and empty tract of space.

'Come back. Come back to me,' the professor's wife whispered as she returned to her tangled bed.

'Come back?' muttered her husband, half-waking once again. 'Is that what you said, darling? But I'm already here, my dear! I'm right here beside you!'

And he sank straight back into sleep.

Every time so far, she reminded herself as she lay there in the darkness, her shadow had come home before sunrise. Its face might be bruised and swollen, its black dress drenched, its feet bare and muddy, but each time it had returned, to be met by her at the back door with anxious, whispered reproaches.

'What took you so long? Can't you see it's nearly dawn?'

She'd hurry it into the kitchen and, after one last furtive peep outside to check that no one had been watching, she would shut the door, bolt it, bolt it again, turn the key in the lock, and begin to ready herself for daylight.

·

But she knew, she already knew, that the morning would one day come when the sun would rise before her shadow had returned. It could be today, it could be tomorrow, it might not be for another month, but on that day, instead of a secret tapping at the back door in the dark, there would be a loud knock at the front door in full daylight, and then a strident ringing of the bell. She'd leap straight from the bed in her haste to answer it before her husband woke. She'd snatch a gown and run downstairs to open the door to the brilliant spotlight of the newly risen sun.

And there, head bowed, the foolish thing would be standing, flanked by stern-eyed swans in policemen's hats, with truncheons dangling beneath their wings. All the creatures of the lake would be crowded at her gate behind them, whispering and murmuring as they savoured the scandalous scene, helpfully lit up for them, as if in some enormous theatre, by the dazzling sunlight from across the water.

'Well, isn't that typical?' the gander would jeer, pushing to the front in his trilby hat, as the watching animals and birds, depending on their kind, quacked or croaked or honked with disapproval and malicious delight. 'Isn't that just typical? They're oh so high and mighty, they're oh so la-de-da, but look what they're *really* like when you see behind the mask!'

And she knew that, when that day came, and her mild, bewildered, boyish husband, the professor, stumbled downstairs in his dressing gown to find out what was going on, it would be *her* standing outside there with her head hanging in shame, *her* between the policemen, *her* in the black dress drenched by the lake, with her hair all tangled and mud between her painted toes. The only shadow she'd have would be the one beside the professor, cast by the low sun, and stretching in from her own muddy feet across the threshold and the hallway floor, to zigzag away up the stairs.

It was still not dawn. Yet from far off to the east she could already hear the tide of clamouring birds.

Creation

It's April, the air is mild as cream and I'm sitting at my front window in a suburban street, tapping the keyboard of my laptop.

Right opposite me is a primary school. Children are running about behind a spiked iron fence. And in the middle of the playground, between the fence and the school, is a magnificent flowering cherry tree.

Masses of white blossom! Pure and bright as heaven!

The pleasant purr of a passing car.

You are here too. A few houses along from me, waiting in your front room for a taxi, looking out at the sunny street.

And walking past your window on the opposite side of the road, Julian Smart appears, the Artist, slender, amused and clean-shaven, in a neat brown coat. To your surprise you discover you can see his thoughts, displayed in a bubble over his head.

'Must get going again,' thinks Julian. 'It's been too long!'

And then another bubble appears.

'Wow, look at *that*!'

They are face to face. On one side of the school railings the Artist looking in. On the other the cherry tree in all its pure white brilliance.

Again you see Julian's thoughts:

'Cherry blossom?! What am I? *Alfred Sisley?*'

Whoosh. Another car.

Mr Veronwy Roberts, the headmaster (a short, plump Welshmen with a round head and bushy eyebrows), is passing the time of day at the front of the school with a pretty young supply teacher named Wendy.

They notice the man in the raincoat looking in over the railing.

'Well, why not though?' Julian is thinking. 'When you come to think about it, why not? Just a question of finding a different *angle*.'

But though you can see his thoughts, Mr Roberts and Wendy can't.

'?' thinks Mr Roberts.

'I'll sort this,' says Wendy, striding firmly over.

'Excuse me. Can I *help* you in any way?'

Julian gives her a dazzling smile.

'You can, I'm sure, in at least a *hundred* ways. But listen, *listen*. I've fallen in love with that tree!'

'And I with you,' thinks Wendy with a sigh. 'And I with you.'

•

Back in his studio Julian Smart gets to work on the phone.

'Hello, Liz! Julian here.' He's standing by the window. 'It's about that *grant money*. I think I've got an idea…'

'Hello, Julian here …' (Now he's sitting at a desk.)

'Hello, is this Acme Tree Surgery?' He's standing again, in another room, lighting a cigarette, with the phone propped under his chin. 'My name is Julian Smart. I wonder if you can give me some *advice*?'

Somewhere across the city, a Gnarled Woodman stands leaning on his van: 'No, you'd need a *specialist contractor* for that. It's a big job. Very tricky.'

The Artist passes his hand over his hair.

'Hello,' he says, 'my name is Julian Smart…'

He's interrupted by the doorbell, and goes to open it with the phone still tucked under his chin. It's Wendy standing outside, looking even prettier than before. He signals to her to come right in and pour herself a drink.

Later, while she reclines naked on his bed looking through a catalogue of his work, he picks up the phone again.

'Hello, is this St Philip's School? Mr Roberts? You're still at work! The teacher's life, eh? This is Julian Smart. The artist? We spoke briefly this morning? …'

A year goes by.

•

In an Art Gallery, people are gathered for a new exhibition. There are canapés, champagne flutes, catalogues. An Elegant Woman is speaking to an Academic of some kind, who wears John Lennon glasses and a leather jacket.

'I just had a peek in the main gallery,' she says. 'Julian's piece is just *fantastic*!'

Behind them an Eminent Critic is inspecting a small work labelled: 'Susan Finchley. *Unfinished Story (7).*' We see the back of the Critic's head, the outside edge of the frame, and the label beside it.

'Hmm,' say his thoughts in the bubble above his head. 'Narrative yet to begin or narrative strangled at birth? Not very original but I'd better be careful, because knowing Susan that's probably the *point.*'

The Elegant Woman stands face to face with another of Susan Finchley's works. Behind, in the distance, framed on one side by the Elegant Woman's profile and on the other by the frame of Finchley's piece, stand two members of the Metropolitan Elite, a man and a woman, each holding a champagne glass.

'Ingenious, I suppose,' the Elegant Woman is thinking, 'but a bit B list, really. Like all of Susan's stuff.'

'With her usual acerbic wit…' The Eminent Critic is already drafting his review in his mind as he moves from one artwork to the next. '… Finchley subverts our received assumptions about originality, about *seriousness*. And yet…'

•

Through the door of the next room an Admiring Group, champagne flutes in hand, can be seen standing in front of a large exhibit, which itself remains hidden from our sight.

'Absolutely breath-taking!' mutters a Man with a Beard.

'Quite extraordinary!' exclaims a Very Thin Woman.

Well, so it should be! Because – look! – it's nothing less than the cherry tree itself, its roots contained in an enormous hemisphere of earth, its branches laden with thick clouds of pure white blossom.

'Julian Smart,' reads the label on the stand in front of it. '*Creation.*'

Julian and the Elegant Woman stand nearby. He wears a fetching but slightly rumpled suit and a very satisfied expression.

'Talk about upstaged,' the Elegant Woman remarks, with a small acidic smile. 'Susan must be *livid.*'

He laughs. 'I hope so. You wouldn't *believe* how much effort went into this. And the *idiots* I've had to deal with!'

Standing to Julian's left and two or three paces behind him, is Wendy, looking very attractive and a little nervous. She is talking to the Academic in John Lennon glasses.

'Oh I *can* believe it,' says the Elegant Woman, 'I assure you of that. You don't work in arts administration without learning what it's like to deal with idiots. But tell me more about it. I'm fascinated by the process.'

Julian glances back at Wendy, sees she's busy talking.

'Well, if you're really interested, why don't you come *over* sometime and I'll tell you the whole story.'

Over against the wall is a small group of other teachers from the school, clustered for protection around the diminutive figure of Mr Veronwy Roberts. They look dowdy and uncomfortable in this place, clutching their glasses of champagne.

But here comes the Eminent Critic.

He sees the tree, looks across at Julian, and smiles, *getting the joke at once.*

Julian strides across to meet him. Laughing as they arrive at the same idea together, they shake hands in front of the tree like Livingstone and Stanley.

Later, back at home, the Eminent Critic sits working on his laptop at his kitchen table.

'*Creation,*' he types, 'is easily this year's most arresting new work. Ostensibly – and indeed *ostentatiously* – silent, it does in fact speak eloquently to us, sharply interrogating (with Smart's characteristic astringency) the idea of "nature" as something prior to and outside of social discourse. Smart has deliberately chosen the most tritely conventional of subjects – cherry blossom – and has transformed it into a complex, maddeningly ambiguous statement precisely by *not transforming it at all*!'

As he continues to tap at his keyboard you can see on the screen the following text, under a standard Microsoft toolbar:

'by insisting on his own complete absence, Smart, almost teasingly, invites us to question what precisely it is that makes this work so unmistakably and triumphantly a work of art. The caption? The gallery setting? The funding – both from public and private sources – that made the work possible? The fact that Julian Smart is a recognised artist? The'

He takes a break in mid-sentence, wandering across his large and well-stocked kitchen to pour himself a glass of red wine. As he stands sipping at it, he flips idly through the TV guide from Saturday's paper. He is still thinking in prose.

'But that only opens up *another* whole line of questioning, of course. What *makes* Julian Smart an artist? Who gave him this licence?... *Mmm, must watch that. Last episode too*... Ultimately it is critics who are the arbiters. Indeed it is perfectly possible to argue that *we* are the actual *creators* of art.'

Stark shadows give his face a certain mythic quality, like the famous poster of Che Guevara, though nothing like as handsome.

Two weeks after the show, on a frosted door marked 'Headmaster' the pot-bellied silhouette of Mr Roberts holds the receiver of a phone in one hand, the rest of the phone in the other, while the coiled flex dangles in between.

'Is this Mr Julian Smart? Yes? Well, we're not happy, Mr Smart. We are not happy about this at all. The agreement was that the tree would be returned *unharmed*!'

Inside the room he is pacing about with beads of sweat on his forehead. Behind him are shelves lined with lever arch files with labels like 'Literacy Strategy', 'Sex Education Guidelines' and 'Promoting Creativity'.

You can see the tree in the playground through the window.

'Our parents are very distressed. Many of them grew up with that tree themselves…'

From the far side of the metal railings you can just see Mr Roberts' upper half as he paces his office.

In front of him is the tree, completely bare, apart from a few shrivelled leaves.

'…would never have agreed in the first place…' he's saying.

A jet passes overhead.

'Well, I'm sorry, mate, but there's absolutely nothing I can do.'

Julian Smart is sitting at a table outside a café. He looks defiantly across at Wendy as he slips his phone back into his jacket pocket.

·

'What does he think I am? Some kind of plant resurrectionist?'

Smartly Dressed Professionals chat at the tables around them. Cars and pedestrians hurry by.

'And what a ridiculous fuss anyway! Anyone would think I'd murdered one of the *kids*.'

Wendy's face looks troubled. 'Yes but…'

'Oh for Christ's sake, don't *you* start! It was only a bloody tree. There are trees everywhere. But just for a moment there that particular tree got to be a unique and famous *work of art*.'

We see Julian's lean and handsome face reflected in the window of the café. A single thought hovers in the bubble above him.

'And there are pretty women everywhere too.'

Mr Roberts sits down wearily at his desk, passing his hand over his face.

I stand with my back to my window watching my story churn out of the printer.

Your doorbell rings.

Transients

There was a delicious, agonising goodbye in Ellie's car, with gentle hands, and moonhoney, and lips still warm from the night, but at last reluctantly they had to heed the honking taxis and the shouting man.

The car door closed. Space and time opened up between them. Thomas watched Ellie rejoin the stream, waved and blew kisses, then turned to hurry into the station, feeling for his ticket in his jacket pocket.

'I really must catch this train,' he'd told her. 'I wish I could stay longer with you, I truly do, but I need to be there for this meeting.'

And yet, when it turned out he'd got the time wrong and that his train was already pulling away, he found he didn't care that much about the meeting, or mind that the hour and a half he now had to wait would be on his own when it could have been with Ellie. He phoned his work to apologise – really it was no big deal at all – then bought some coffee and sat on a kind of gallery above the platforms, under Victorian arches of iron and glass, with four or five big intercity trains beneath him, lying side by side beneath their power lines like metal whales.

What could be better than the solitude of a railway station at half past 9 in the morning, he thought? It was beautiful as a cathedral, but a cathedral whose god was real and performed miracles many times in every hour. It was a temple of power and speed.

The caffeine lit him up, transforming his veins into branching fingers of contentment. He watched the pigeons, the electric trolleys, a giant electric advertising hoarding that changed every ten seconds: girl – car – beach – cartoon rabbit – girl – car – beach – cartoon rabbit…

Another train came hissing to a standstill right below him. For two seconds it just stood there, and then suddenly, all along its flank, doors slid simultaneously open to disgorge a crowd of people with bags, suitcases, baby buggies, bicycles, who began at once to hurry towards the city. In poured another crowd, equally keen to get away.

For some reason, the image came into his mind of a great sphere hanging up there at the mouth of the station where the trains came and went. One side of the sphere was in sunlight where he couldn't see it, the other within the shadow of the station roof.

10.58! Jane jumped out of a taxi with a badly packed bag in her hand. Oh for God's sake keep the bloody change then, you crook. Which bloody platform? Which bloody train? Why don't they fix that bloody departure board? God damn it if I have to sit around

here and wait for the next train I swear I'll bloody
kill someone.

She was *angry*. She was riding a great red horse
with teeth of steel and people had better stand
back because it could bite and kick and shoot out
gamma rays from its hell-fire eyes. Platform 9! Okay,
now *run*. She'd finally done it after threatening it
so many times that she herself ceased to believe in
it. She'd ditched the bastard, she had crawled out
of the hole, she'd let the red horse loose from the
catacomb where it had champed in the darkness for
so long. And, look, it was twelve feet tall, strong as a
tank, lethal as a bloody bomb.

'Hurry up please, miss, we're about to go.'

I am fucking hurrying, you stupid man. I am in
fact running as you may possibly have observed.

And *don't* call me 'miss'.

God will you *look* at this shower in here with their
smartphones and their bloody tablets.

Where am I going to sit?

Miss. Patronising git. *Miss*. What does he know
about my marital status? Mind you he's right. I *am*
single now. I'm bloody single and that's the way it's
going to stay for a long long time.

No, mate, I am *not* going to sit by you, you look
as if the art of washing is one that you have not yet
mastered.

No, madam, you may be very nice, but my red
horse doesn't like you and I fear it might bite your
big soft ears.

Single!

No, certainly not you, your reverence. Anyone who munches sandwiches with their mouth open like that should be doomed for all eternity to sit alone. Nor you either, kind sir. I make it a golden rule in life never to sit with people who look at my tits and visibly salivate.

The train began to move as she passed on to the next carriage.

Settled at a window seat facing forward with a whole table to himself, Thomas checked his phone. It was odd, now he thought about it, that it had never occurred to him to do this during all the time he'd been sitting on that gallery watching the trains. It was even odder that, after making the call to work to say he'd be late, he'd set his phone to silent.

Sure enough, there were three separate messages from Ellie.

'Missing you but VERY happy.'

'Can't wait till the weekend.'

'I love you SO much, Thomas, I can hardly stand it.'

He looked down at them coldly. It was impossible to deny it any more: that thing that always happened had happened again. He'd really believed it wouldn't this time, he'd really believed that this was a different case entirely, but it had happened. He could remember having feelings. He could remember having very powerful ones as he said goodbye to her outside the

station, but now, looking down at her texts, he felt…
what? Embarrassment. Guilt. Shame. And something else that could almost be called revulsion.

He'd foolishly encouraged another sentient
entity to transform itself into the excited bundle of
hope and need that had sent him these three texts,
no doubt hoping to provoke a similar excitement
in himself, and to elicit texts in return in a cycle of
mutual affirmation. But the idea of their having
become a couple now just seemed distasteful and
bizarre. She was a stranger to him, as much of a
stranger as the various other passengers who were
settling themselves down in the carriage around
him, stowing bags, opening laptops, fiddling with
phones. All that had happened was that she had
briefly worn that mask he sometimes handed out:
the Object of Love, the Object of Desire, the One
Who Is So Like Me that I Need Not Be Alone.

That stupid mask. When King Midas embraced a
woman she turned to gold, but, for him, it was the
other way round. What had briefly seemed golden
became… well… just *this*. No wonder he'd silenced
his phone. Since he'd called his office to say he was
going to miss the meeting, he'd really not thought
of Ellie at all. Well, he'd not thought of anyone. Why
would he, when he'd been so entirely content by
himself?

Oh lord, he thought, this is terrible. I'm going
to have to call her now, aren't I, and say this was all
a mistake?

He could see the hurt he'd cause. He felt pretty badly about it already, and knew he'd soon feel worse, but he was still somewhat cushioned. For there were few places in the world that seemed safer and more comforting to Thomas than a train that was about to leave the station.

Perhaps I'm just not cut out for this whole relationship business at all, he thought. It really wasn't as if he ever acted cynically, or ever set out deliberately to deceive. He wanted to experience love, or thought he did, and so he sought it out, persuading himself over and over that he'd really found it.

He thought of the sphere, that great sphere he'd imagined hanging there at the mouth of the station. It was supposed to stop, that was the thing. You were supposed to choose one side and let the other go. But he didn't know how to make that happen. The side he thought he'd picked just kept turning until it had disappeared from sight, and a new blank face turned towards him.

The train, the long clean train, which at first had seemed such a haven, suddenly felt oppressively warm. Thomas stood up to take off his jacket and, as he did so, Jane came into his carriage from the one behind it. The train jolted as she came alongside him, in the way that trains do as they are getting into their stride, and the two of them tottered and nearly fell into one another.

Both laughed, and each of them looked

appreciatively, just for a moment, directly into the other's eyes. They were a good-looking pair.

Perhaps a woman like this would be more his type, Thomas found himself thinking. A bit spikier than Ellie. More challenging. A little less comforting warmth, but much more fire.

He looks interesting, Ellie said to herself. And then she thought: I could just turn towards him and start chatting him up right now, if I felt like it. I could flirt outrageously if I wanted to. There's nothing to stop me. I've got no ties any more. I can do whatever I like.

Later, when the train had been under way for twenty minutes, Thomas went to the little lobby at the end of the carriage to find some privacy for his difficult call.

'It's all moving a bit too fast for me,' he'd decided he'd say, selecting a well-used phrase from the standard lexicon. 'I just think we need to pause a bit and take stock.'

That would be enough for the moment, wouldn't it? It would buy him some time and prepare the ground as gently as possible for more. And, after all, he couldn't be sure that this wasn't really the case. Maybe they *were* moving too fast. If the sphere could turn once, perhaps it would come back round again in due course, and maybe even this time come to rest? Who could say whether how he was feeling now would prove any more permanent than how he'd felt in Ellie's car?

Perhaps this sudden coldness I feel is really just panic, he said to himself. Like people freeze up after accidents and things like that. They go numb, don't they? They know what's happened but they can't experience it, because it's just too much to process. Which wasn't so different, now he came to think about it, from a computer freezing when you asked it to do too many things at once. If he and Ellie slowed down a bit, and he felt more in control again – who knows? – those feelings might all come back.

It was always a bonus, if the things you said were actually true.

But none of these thoughts stopped him, as he took out his phone, from leaning forward a little so he could see, through the glass door and down the carriage, the red-haired woman with the fiery eyes.

Jane saw him look at her and turned away. Her initial elation had already faded. It no longer seemed to her, as it had done only a few minutes previously, that anything was possible, or that somehow, magically, she had ended an alliance that had lasted more than two years, and yet escaped the price to be paid in loneliness and grief. And what had seemed, when she entered this carriage, to be the elation of freedom, now looked in retrospect more like hysteria or shock. A kind of dazed blankness had replaced it now, but grief would soon follow, she knew: bitter, unremitting grief, cold and hard like stone. And then for a long time, for many months quite possibly, she'd have to beat like a prisoner on that cold implacable wall.

There was a ditch running along beside the track. It was separated from the railway by a single low wire, hung between concrete posts. She watched the wire numbly as it disappeared into clumps of vegetation, emerged briefly, and disappeared again, sometimes for many yards at a time. But that bare grey metal always came back in the end, running along by itself next to the train.

When Thomas made his way back down the carriage, his face was taut. He resumed his seat without even glancing at Jane. Ellie had wept and shouted and called him names. He turned to the window, but didn't even register the world outside.

After a time he noticed his own reflection. It was very faint, almost transparent, a wispy, insubstantial thing that was barely there at all.

The Kite

Darius strode across the park on his way to the pub. He was a big man, over six foot tall, solid and broad like the rugby player he'd once been. His great thick mane was just beginning to turn grey, and grey hair spilled out from the open neck of his shirt.

It was a blowy evening. With each new gust of wind, a row of big chestnut trees to Darius's right began to dance, the great round clumps of foliage swaying back and forth across the trunks like the massive breasts and thighs of giant women. Over on his left, beyond the open grass, was the town hospital. All his daughters had been born there, as Darius himself had been, and three of the group of friends he was going to meet that night.

In the middle of the park, a father and his young son were flying a kite. Darius had flown kites here too, when he was a boy himself, and when his own daughters were growing up. The girls had a big red one, he remembered, and the oldest had a pink one of her own with a pony on it that never really worked. This kite now was bright blue. When those big trees began to dance, it strained so hard towards the sky that the father and son together had a struggle to hold it down. Darius remembered how that felt, the string as hard as metal wire. The boy yelled out with excitement at the power he felt in his hands. The dad glanced at Darius and smiled.

The pub was right on the edge of the park. It was called the Live and Let Live, and when those giant tree-women danced and the kite string turned to wire, its sign creaked and swayed on its rusty hinges. In the bright, windy evening, Darius put his hand to the door.

He stepped through into the body of a living creature. Softly lit, humming with activity, pungent with hot meat and fermentation, it was tightly packed with lumps of flesh in many shapes and sizes, some of them oozing bile, others storing fat, others again pumping out the precious fluid on which the entire organism depended.

As Darius looked round for his friends there was a certain weariness in his eyes, but he banished it at once as soon as he spotted them.

'Hello there, fellers, sorry I'm late. Chris was going to drop me off, but then something cropped up for her and I had to walk instead.'

'No worries,' said Roger. 'We've got your pint ready.'

'Room for a small one on the bench there, Bill?' asked Darius. 'Did you see the news this evening? This bloody government just gets worse and worse.'

And then he was off. They were all off, but especially Darius. From their table in the Live and Let Live, he and his friends strode out together across the world, seeking out injustice, absurdity and cant, and flinging it fearlessly aside.

But halfway through his third pint, Darius's mood suddenly changed.

'Look at us. Still drinking in the same old pub we've been coming to since we were fifteen years old. What have we done with our lives, eh, lads? Let's be honest, for all the lot of us have seen and done in this world, we might as well have been canaries in a cage.'

It was an old refrain, but the others tried their best to look interested.

'I could have played for England,' Darius told them, although this wasn't news to any of them. 'I was *good*. I was really good. I had that sports scholarship offered me, remember? I had a career offered me on a plate. But like a fool I turned it down.'

He'd gone to the local college instead, and ended up working as a draughtsman in this same little town, with its park, and its boating lake, and its small but award-winning folk museum.

'A sports career would just have been the beginning, too. You all know how passionate I am about politics. Well, I could have gone down that road. I would have had a platform, wouldn't I? I could have made my mark.'

The others waited stoically, like animals enduring

rain, keeping their minds a blank until the dark clouds pass. They knew Darius, and they knew that sometimes he couldn't feel complete until he'd summoned up this shadow, this alternate self, and brought it to stand beside him.

Outside, darkness fell. The park was empty. The boy and his father had gone home. But the dance of the chestnut trees was constant now, as if those tree-women could hear some urgent drum so deep that it was beyond the reach of human ears. Wisps of wind-torn cloud blew from time to time across the rising moon.

'Of course it's a lot to do with Chris really,' Darius declared. 'Bless her, you couldn't wish for a kinder heart, but she was never the right woman for me. She really wasn't right at all.'

His friends looked uncomfortable. They disliked this part. All of their wives were friends of Chris's, and so indeed were they themselves.

'And by the same token of course,' Darius added hastily, so as not to seem to be putting Chris down, 'I wasn't right for her at all. We were just too young to realise it.'

This was the very heart, as Darius saw it, of all his difficulties. Chris had got pregnant when they were barely more than children themselves, and had needed her parents' support. He'd not felt able to leave her and take up the opportunity he'd been offered, because he'd seen how important it was to her to have her mum round the corner, and her sister a few streets away, and it just wouldn't have been fair to ask her to give that up. And he couldn't walk out on his own child.

But Chris lacked his ambition.

'A home, some kids, a reasonable job, a night out once in a while with her friends, an annual holiday, that's all she asks of life.'

His friends frowned down at their drinks. It was all they asked of life as well. All that most people asked of life, in their experience. What was wrong with that?

Darius sighed, and knocked back the last of his beer.

'It's far too late to worry about it now, I know. I've made my bed and I must lie in it. And, don't get me wrong, it's not such a bad bed as these things go. Chris is a good woman and I've had it easy in all kinds of ways. But if I could have my life again …'

He looked round at their faces and saw that he hadn't brought them with him.

'Sorry, lads. I'm really sorry. I've been a bit of a downer tonight, haven't I? I'm tired, I guess. Haven't been sleeping well. I think maybe I should love you and leave you, if you don't mind. Get an early night. I'll be fine in the morning, and better company next time we meet, but you'll have more fun without me tonight.'

•

'The weird thing,' said Roger, after Darius had gone, 'is that Chris tells a completely different story. It was Darius who suggested the baby in the first place, and it was Darius, not Chris, who was determined they shouldn't move.'

The night was charged with superhuman energy. Countless billions of tons of air were moving rapidly over the town, making pub signs clank and creak and burglar alarms go off in cars. Darius buttoned his coat up to the neck as he strode off across the park. The big trees jived and roared. He felt like some tiny crawling thing at the bottom of the sea, with the waves crashing about above him in the world outside.

And as he walked beneath those great dark crashing waves, a shadow crossed the moon, unseen by him, unseen by anyone at all. It was the Angel of Death, riding the blast on its papery wings as it looked down on the town beneath it with its ancient, empty eyes. It didn't notice the park or the folk museum. It didn't see the trees or the roofs of the houses. All it saw was the souls that were its prey, like little lights in a void.

'You're home early, sweetheart,' murmured Chris sleepily as Darius climbed into the warm space beside her.

'Yeah, a bit tired. Thought I'd call it a night.'

'Nice evening?'

'Oh, you know, bit samey, but they're good blokes, every one of them. Hearts in the right place and all of that.'

'You *are* tired aren't you, poor pet,' she said, cuddling up against him in the darkness.

It was a long time before he slept. He lay with his eyes open for an hour or more, while the wind blew across the chimneys and rattled the front gate, thinking about all the places he could once have gone, that were now beyond his reach.

Two days later, Darius came back to an empty house. Chris was a teaching assistant in a local school and was normally home before he was, but he remembered now that she'd had some sort of social event to go to after work. One of the teachers was retiring, she'd said, or something like that.

'I won't be very late,' she'd said, 'but I will have eaten. I'll leave you to fix something for yourself.'

It always unsettled him, coming home to an empty house, and he could never quite help himself from feeling a certain childish resentment towards Chris for not being there, and towards whoever she was with for keeping her from him. Of course he knew quite well that this was silly and unfair.

He took a bottle of beer from the fridge and went to sit by the fishpond in his garden. The windy weather had passed. It was a calm evening and, as the light faded, the dragonflies came like they sometimes did, dry and papery, buzzing and droning around the water on some mysterious business of their own.

What were they doing, he wondered, these strange archaic creatures that had been here before the dinosaurs, here when the first fish wriggled out onto the land?

He dozed off for a bit. When he woke it was dark, and the doorbell was ringing inside the house.

Cycling home from the retirement do at work, Chris had been hit by a car. She lost consciousness instantly.

People gathered round her. Somebody made a call. The police arrived and an ambulance came whooping through the streets. She was taken to the hospital and laid out on a bed in a special room of her own, surrounded by humming machines. The room had a view of those chestnut trees on the far side of the park. They were hardly moving at all.

When Darius arrived, her doctor told him that they wanted to disconnect her from life support.

'I'm so sorry but I'm afraid she's gone,' the doctor said. 'There's absolutely no brain activity at all.'

Darius, with his lion's mane, began to rage and roar.

'No way!' he bellowed. 'You'll have to kill me first!' He shoved doctors and nurses away from where his wife lay like Sleeping Beauty, her chest peacefully rising and falling. He stood guard in front of her, daring them to come near. 'Look at her, for Christ's sake! Just bloody look at her! She's *obviously* alive!'

It was his three daughters, all of them in their twenties, who finally persuaded him that Chris was no longer present. Her body was just ticking over by itself, they explained to him over and over. It was like an idling vehicle with no one behind the wheel. The driver would never return.

In the early hours of morning, Darius's girls walked their father home across the park. Fresh air will be good for us, they said, trying their best to be grown-up. Two of them supported Darius, as if he was an old man who couldn't stand by himself. And actually he couldn't. It was as if some kind of malignant leech had sucked all the life and blood from him, all the muscle, all the roar.

As they passed under the chestnut trees, the clumps of foliage rustled slightly and sighed above their heads. Entangled among them was the bright blue kite. It had pulled so hard and long towards the sky that its string had finally snapped. And without the tension that had held it firm against the wind, it no longer knew how to fly.

The Steps

1.

'He is your father, Isola,' says Nanny B. 'He is your own papa. We know you haven't seen much of him. But men have business to attend to. He has ten thousand Africans working for him, or so they say.'

'I know he's my father,' scoffs Lady Isola. 'I've seen him lots of times.'

2.

His Lordship sits enthroned in the nursery armchair to receive his kiss. He is grinning like a schoolboy. In a semicircle round him stand the nursery staff, wringing their hands. Isola edges towards the stranger.

'My, but she's a pretty thing, eh?' says Lord Robert. 'We'll have to fight the men off this one.'

There are black pits all over his nose and his eyes have yellow bits in them. His hands clamp tightly onto her legs.

'I have a surprise for you, Isola, but you must come with me to find it.'

3.

Up the stairs, across the landing, along a corridor. They pass faded tapestries of hunters, wild beasts, a screaming horse being savaged by a lion. There is a brown smell of mould and honey.

'Well, we've never been *here* before, have we, Isola!' cries Nanny B.

Up more stairs, across another landing with glass cases packed with tiny iridescent birds which perch on branches, sing, stretch out their wings and fly, though all of them are completely dead.

They come to a little pointed door. It looks like the entrance to a cupboard, but inside is a spiral staircase.

'What funny little steps, Isola!' exclaims Nanny B. 'How many are there, I wonder? Why don't we count them? One, two, three ...'

His Lordship opens the door at the top.

'Thirty-three!' cries Nanny B.

4.

They're in a small octagonal room inside a tower, with seven windows and one door.

Through the windows Isola can see other towers, empty as this one, a square kilometre of leaded roofs, and the four gold balls above the façade in the distance.

Inside the room there is a small round table with two chairs. There is also a leather armchair, with an ashtray beside it on a column of brass.

'My late wife called this the Dolorous Tower,' his Lordship tells Nanny B, referring to Isola's mother. 'Ha, ha. Always the romantic.'

On the table are a glass of lemonade and a plate of chocolates, each decorated with a crystallised fruit. Also a box tied up with ribbon.

5.

His Lordship dismisses Nanny B.

'Why don't you sit down and eat the chocolates, Isola?'

The chocolates taste stale.

'Come on then, drink! Drink the lemonade!'

Lord Robert lights a cigar. He is restless. He feels in his pockets for his watch and then for a silver hip flask. He takes a swig and his eyes go red and watery.

'Open your present, Isola. I brought it for you all the way from Africa.'

She pulls the box towards her and starts to pull and tug at the ribbon.

'You'll never do it at that rate.'

Irritably, Lord Robert tosses his cigar into the ashtray, takes out a pocket knife with an ivory handle, and rips through the ribbon with a single upward jerk.

6.

Inside is the most hideous object Isola has ever seen. It is a golden goblet with a golden base, but its pedestal is a wrist and a hand. Not a pretend hand of gold or ivory, but an actual hand, the hand of an enormous hairy man, with real skin and real nails, its thumb and fingers reaching up almost to the rim.

She is only six. She gives a small, appalled gasp.

Her father laughs.

'You think it's a *human* hand, don't you, you silly child? Of course it isn't. It's the hand of a wild beast. A fierce gorilla. Your brave Papa shot it himself from a river steamer.'

'Thank you, Papa,' Isola manages at last to say.

'You don't think your papa would chop off the hands of a *person*, do you, Isola? That would be a *very* bad thing to do.'

7.

'Now then, Isola,' says his Lordship sternly, looking at his watch, 'I must be going soon.'

He leans toward her, though he looks not at her eyes, but at the top of her head.

'Let's make this our special room, eh, Isola? Our secret room. You can leave that funny old gorilla cup up here if you want. It will be here for you when we come up again.'

He sits back in his armchair.

'One more kiss for your dear papa who buys you expensive presents.'

He looks at Isola's chin.

'That's real gold, you know,' he says. 'Real African gold. You must kiss me on the mouth.'

Isola does not like the steely way his hands clamp

onto her so that only he can choose the time for her to move away. But even less she likes how his cigar-tasting tongue comes suddenly pushing and poking between her lips.

But then he goes back to Africa, disappearing into the map on the nursery wall.

8.

Isola is at her dolls' house. The dolls have been having a banquet, a wonderful feast, with plaster chicken, and plaster roast beef, and three different colours of plaster blancmange. But now they fall silent so that Isola can listen to the nursery maids.

'Yes. Late last night,' says one. 'Karl said he was in one of his moods and hit poor Claude with a riding crop.'

'Up drinking till the early hours I heard,' the other says. 'Moaning and groaning away about inter-fering do-gooders and no gratitude and all his good work undone.'

'Things have gone bad for him over there, appar-ently,' the first one says. 'He's lost his position or something like that. That's why he's back so soon.'

9.

Isola pretends to nibble at the English biscuits which her father has laid out next to the severed hand.

She finds it hard to understand his mood. His speech is slurred and his eyes red. He looks at her chin rather than her eyes, and talks about do-gooders and bleeding hearts. He says he is misunderstood and all alone in the world. At one point it seems to Isola he might be crying, though it is so unlike her own crying that she can't be sure. She is only seven.

Then he says, 'Come and kiss me, my dear little Isola. You are all I have in the world.'

10.

Isola kisses her Papa.

Still he doesn't look her in the face. She can tell that there is something about her that interests him but it doesn't seem to have anything to do with what looks out of her eyes.

'Don't try to close your mouth,' he snaps. 'No one wants a girl who won't open up.'

11.

His Lordship's face is red and agitated.

'Each other is all we have left in the world, Isola. All we have in the world.'

His gaze moves from her chin to the top of her head, and then away, across the room. He seems to disintegrate in some way. And she does too. She turns herself into a cloud of little specks of dust that have no feelings and mean nothing to anyone at all. So thoroughly does she disassemble herself, in fact, that it comes as a shock to notice that her father is once more speaking to her, as if she were present and real.

'Did you notice that funny lumpy thing I've got in my trousers?' he murmurs, speaking so stealthily that it is as if he himself is trying to avoid hearing it. 'I bet you wondered what it was.'

He pulls her hand across. But as soon as she touches it he jumps up from his chair, as if the touch was an unwelcome and intrusive act initiated by her.

'You must never, never, ever tell anyone what happens in this tower, do you understand?' he thunders. 'Never.'

12.

She is back in the Tower again. The table is bare. Lord Robert locks the door with a shaky hand then pulls her over to the chair.

'Did you keep your promise? Did you tell no one?'

'Yes, Papa, no one.'

'Good girl, good girl,' he whispers, looking away from her, as if he himself doesn't wish to hear what he's about to say. 'Well now, I'm going to let you see it!'

Nothing has prepared Isola for what now comes springing out of his unbuttoned fly. It is gnarled and wrinkly like a tree, with blue tubes in it, and an ugly, blind little mouth.

His Lordship's hand shoots out and clamps around her wrist.

'It wants you to stroke it.'

She has hardly touched it before it spits over the front of her dress.

'Damn!' shouts her father, leaping up. 'God damn it!'

13.

Small Isola alone in the high dark corridors, with their smell of mould and honey. Behind her an embroidered jaguar sinks its teeth into the neck of a tapir, while at the same time a giant snake coils round the jaguar, so as to crush it to death. But she isn't looking at the tapestries or the dead animals' heads. She's keeping her mind as empty as she can.

14.

'You are not to tell anyone. Not *anyone*, do you understand, or Papa will be very very cross.'

His gaze has been roving round the room. Suddenly he picks up the gorilla goblet and a gleam comes into his eyes.

'You know I told you your Papa would never cut off a person's hand? Well, I'll tell you the truth now, Isola. It's different in Africa. We cut people's hands off all the time. It's the only language those darkies understand. Oh yes, Isola, me and my men have cut off many hands, even from little girls like you.'

15.

Isola is at her dolls' house in the nursery. The dolls are burying a child. She mutters and whispers to them crossly while her ears strain to hear what Nanny is saying to a maid. Four years have passed since she first visited the Tower and she is ten years old.

'We can all see it, Francine, not just you, and we are all distressed. But remember we're only servants.

There is nothing we can do.'

Nanny B comes over to Isola.

'Isola, your father has sent us word…'

Still facing her dolls, Isola flinches. Then she turns a blank face to her nanny and awaits instruction.

16.

Isola in the corridor of silent humming birds, wearing a red dress.

'Nothing happened,' she is telling herself, 'nothing important. I can't even remember. No, no, I really can't remember a *thing.'*

There is a painting above her of an eagle devouring a dove.

17.

Back in the nursery, the servants rush forward, but she turns away from them.

'I think I'd like to play with my dolls.'

18.

Isola in a blue dress with ribbons in her hair, passing the dead humming birds in their glass case.

19.

Isola at the bottom of the thirty-three steps. She opens the lower door and steps out into the corridor. As always, there's no one there. Only dead animals, and pictures of animals dying.

20.

Isola in white at fourteen years, passing a suit of armour on an upper landing.

'I really don't remember,' says the pale girl to herself, 'I really don't remember at all.'

21.

From out of the ornamental pool at the front of the palace, six stone horses draw a marble charioteer.

Regiments of poplar trees frame the grassy avenue that leads from the chariot to a column on the ridge of the hill. On top of the column is a human form made of stone. It is the dead wife of the first Duke, set high above the Earth against the sky.

The poplar trees are pale yellow, like white wine.

The leaves slowly fall.

22.

In mirrored alcoves, young women giggle with bewhiskered gentlemen. A violinist plays a sentimental tune. Outside it is autumn again and, far away in her palace, Isola has just turned sixteen.

Two gentlemen sit at the bar.

'You're just like I used to be,' Lord Robert is telling his new friend.

How old he looks with his lank grey hair, his cheeks puffy and purple and hatched with broken veins. His companion is only just twenty, with a moustache so thin that it's barely worth the name. His blue eyes are full of resentment and doubt.

'You should have seen me when I was your age, Henri,' says Lord Robert. 'Full of energy! Full of fire! I was running a concession half the size of this whole damn country, would you believe, getting useful work out of ten thousand good-for-nothing darkies. And then the busy-bodies came and ruined it all, God damn it. But, my dear young friend – and I do *mean* friend, though we have only just met – my dear, dear friend, I implore you, don't be like me. Don't ever let them take away your dreams!'

'But no one buys my paintings,' complains Henri. 'No one offers me commissions. No one appreciates my art.'

'*I* will commission you,' says Lord Robert grandly.

He rises unsteadily to his feet, warily watched by the young women in the mirrors.

'You shall come to my palace,' he proclaims, so loudly that all the room can hear him, 'and you will paint the world a masterpiece. I'll provide you with everything you need. You'll paint my lake and my house and my fine park. And when you've done that, you'll paint me. Yes, me, in the medal awarded me by the King himself.'

He draws on his cigar while tears well up in his eyes. Then he sinks back down onto his seat, picks up his brandy and adds with a grudging little shrug:

'You can even paint my daughter, I suppose, but you'll have to add a little flesh to her bones.'

23.

Isola watches Henri as he begins to make sketches. She sees him glance uneasily at the immaculate finish of the oil paintings on the walls. She can see he's frightened. She can tell he's completely out of his depth.

'Don't worry,' she says, 'by the time Papa gets back from Africa, he'll have forgotten he even asked you.'

She doesn't pity Henri exactly, or find him attractive, but she is oddly fascinated by his fear.

'I'm not really a landscape painter,' he says, 'but I would love to draw pictures of you.'

Soon he's given up painting altogether and is pouring his energies instead, at every opportunity, into Isola's listless but pliant body.

When she tells him she's pregnant, he disappears.

24.

Lady Isola, in her four-poster bed, cradles the new baby.

Her eyes see nothing but the small and squirming thing. Her ears hear nothing but its snorting and snuffling. And indeed she sniffs and snuffles herself, for her nose can't ever seem to get enough of its warm and biscuity smell.

'Amanda, I will call her,' she tells Nanny B. 'It means lovable, you know.'

25.

It is Amanda's seventh birthday, and here is Isola in the nursery armchair with her daughter's present in her lap.

She's found that she can't cope for more than a very short time with the unruly demands of a child, but she still visits her nearly every week. Officially, of course, Amanda is an orphan, and Isola is the little girl's *guardian*.

Amanda approaches the armchair to collect the small parcel. She is quite fond of her mother, but a little shy. Nanny B and her staff stand watching, wringing their hands in unison, as they will the little girl to be pleased.

Amanda unwraps the parcel. Her mother has bought her a beautiful little hairpin, ornamented with a heart picked out in tiny rubies and diamonds. Amanda smiles and shows it to her staff, though she would have preferred a toy.

26.

Isola waits at the nursery door, while Amanda is being wrapped up for a walk.

'But where is the hairpin?' she asks. 'She hasn't worn it the last two times I saw her. Does she not like it any more?'

'Oh no, your Ladyship, she loves the pin. It's just that she might lose it in the park.'

'Oh nonsense, I can keep an eye on it. Fetch it for her now. I'd like to see it again.'

Nanny B draws breath.

'Your Ladyship, please don't be distressed, but I have to confess it's gone astray. We were hoping to find it quickly and spare your Ladyship the upset.'

'Spare me the upset? You've lied to me and you've lost my gift, and yet you speak of *sparing* me? It was a heart! Did you notice that? It was in the shape of a heart! What are you going to do next? Rip me open and tear the real heart from my body? Probably you'd love to. You've never cared for me one bit.'

27.

Fat and middle-aged at twenty-four, Isola trudges heavily along the corridor of silent birds. She has set every servant searching for the hairpin, and now she's scouring the palace herself, looking for hiding places that the servants might have missed.

And here, unexpectedly, is the door to the Tower. She stands and looks at it, not consciously recognising it, but puzzled by a sudden *absence* in her mind. Like a page missing in

28.

The smell of cigar smoke, the table, the armchair, the hideous goblet. It all comes back to her – it always did, every time she came here – and she wonders, as always, how she could ever have forgotten something so large and so terrible.

But this is the first time she's ever been here alone. She can smell the lingering remnants of her father's cigar smoke but Lord Robert himself has gone to the capital, and isn't expected to return for several weeks. This means that, unlike every previous time she came through this door, Isola faces no new onslaught, nothing to pull her attention away from the memories stored here in this octagonal room with its seven windows, the memories that—

But then suddenly she sees it! The missing hairpin! It's lying beside the armchair on the floor!

Everything becomes clear in a single moment. He has been bringing Amanda here. He has been bringing her here for the past year. That's why he leaves Isola alone.

With a cry, she runs to the stairs.

29.

Less than half a minute later she emerges from the lower door into the corridor of dead birds. She is confused. In thirty-three steps she has completely forgotten what it was that so agitated her, but her heart is still pounding, and her palms are still clammy with sweat.

'Why am I in such a state?' she wonders.

Then she looks down at her hand.

'I suppose I must be excited I've found this,' she thinks, seeing the little jewelled pin.

30.

The whole palace is a dolls' house like the one in the nursery. It has tiny rooms and tiny corridors, and miniature people are distributed among them, performing their various tasks.

At the top, in the Dolorous Tower, are the tiny figures of Amanda and her grandfather, his hand under her skirt.

Far below them is Amanda's mother, Isola, by herself, plodding heavily through the dim brown corridors.

The stairs between Isola and the Tower are mostly empty. Here and there the occasional tiny servant hurries on some errand this way or that, but none of them are carrying messages between Isola and her child.

31.

But here at last is Isola back in the corridor of birds. A year has gone by since she was last here and she has no idea why she's come, or what has made her wanderings through the palace become so much more extreme and agitated as time has passed.

She finds herself in front of the door to the Tower. Again she notices her own startling lack of any feeling, as one might notice a sentence which

32.

Back in the Tower itself, she recalls everything, and this time she understands something new.

'If I leave the Tower,' she realises, 'I will instantly forget again.'

It is like an enchantment that she put upon herself long ago when she was a little child, to protect the rest of her life, as best she could, from being swallowed up by the Dolorous Tower.

She goes to the windows. Most of them look out over empty rooftops but on one side, to the left of the door, one of them looks down into a small stone courtyard adjoining some pantries. It is a bright winter day, but the courtyard is in shadow, as it almost always is. And down there, far below her, as if at the bottom of a well, two servants are beating a carpet.

The window doesn't open, so Isola bangs as hard as she can on the thick glass. But she's too far up. They wouldn't be able to hear her, even if they weren't hitting that carpet so energetically.

She turns back into the room, her eyes darting round that small, accursed space, until they alight on the gorilla goblet that still sits there on the table. At once Isola snatches it up, grasping the hairy skin which has always revolted her, as if it were the hand of a friend.

She strikes it against the glass with all her strength.

The window smashes and her whole arm goes through, while the gorilla goblet, flying from her plump fingers, falls down the middle of that stony well to smash into three pieces at the feet of the astonished servants.

Isola sticks her head out of the broken window.

'You! Come at once! Bring whoever you can!'

33.

Mouths wide open, the servants look down at the strange objects scattered on the flagstones: a golden disk, a golden cup and a single huge black hand.

Then they look up, squinting into the small square of blue above them. They are amazed to see Lady Isola up there, bellowing like a bull into the bright, cold air. She is normally so fat and so sleepy.

'You! Come here!' commands Isola. 'Bring paper and something to write with.'

They assume she's gone mad, of course, but she *is* the daughter of the Duke. Dropping their beaters, they run to obey.

Frozen Flame

Only recently has it occurred to me that Nicola was also young. She was nine years older than me, and at the time she seemed wonderfully knowing and grown-up, with a husband and kids and everything, but she was only twenty-eight.

She was a mature student on the same course as me at Bristol Poly. We got talking one day, in the little café attached to the library, about a coursework project we'd been set, and we agreed to meet again from time to time to support each other. I assumed she'd latched onto me because she thought I'd be useful to her. I was a very bright student and, though she was very able herself, she'd left school at sixteen and hadn't played the academic game for a long time. So I guessed it was me that was going to help her, and not the other way round, but I was perfectly happy to play along, just for the pleasure of her company. She was lively, full of irreverent energy, and very quick to laugh and smile. She also swore a lot and, in seminars, she and another mature student, her terrifyingly beautiful friend Fay, spoke about sex in a frank and matter-of-fact way which I found fascinating and disturbing in equal measure, a window into a world which I longed to inhabit but had no idea how to reach.

It was the third time I met with Nicola, this time in a little hippie place a mile or so from the campus, that I first realised there was more to this than just helping her with her coursework. We'd met at 11, and, after two cups of coffee, had got to 12 o'clock without even mentioning the project. I was a creature of doubt, but even I had to admit to myself that there was really no doubt about it: an attractive, properly grown-up woman was enjoying my company for its own sake. She even laughed at my jokes.

Nicola seemed to notice some change in my face as I registered this, for she smiled, reached over and lightly cupped her hand over mine.

'We're two of a kind in some ways, aren't we?' she said.

Two of a kind! Spoken to this very shy young man who had spent years worrying if he'd ever manage to negotiate a relationship with any woman at all, that phrase was like a shot of heroin into a main artery! Up to that point, I'd known that I liked Nicola and of course I'd known that I found her very attractive too (although this was true of several other women on the course, including Nicola's friend Fay), but from that moment onwards, I was utterly and desperately in love.

When you look out into the world you can't see your own face. All you see is a kind of frame round the edge of your field of vision, with, somewhere towards the bottom of it, a shadowy out-of-focus blob that's the tip of your nose. I often had the feeling back then that this absence of a face wasn't just the result of my particular perspective, but was the actual case. I really didn't *have* a face, in other words. Other people could look straight in, much as you might look in through the window of some psychic washing machine, and see the tangle of anxiety and shame and frustrated desire that was whirling round inside. So I felt this burst of gratitude and love, but then I panicked. Fearing that Nicola could see straight into my head, I looked quickly away from her to avoid her gaze, and realised to my dismay that I was blushing violently.

'Oh Rick, I'm so sorry! I didn't mean to embarrass you!' Her hand was still resting on mine, and she gave it a reassuring squeeze. 'It's just that it's a very long time since I laughed so much, or felt so comfortable in anyone else's company.'

I made myself look at her again. Her brown eyes were warm and kind. She wasn't mocking me, I could see. She didn't think any less of me for having blushed. Incredible as it might seem, Nicola didn't just see tangled wet stuff churning round when she looked at me, but an actual face with eyes and nose and mouth, which for some strange reason she'd grown to like. She'd always looked pretty to me, but now she had suddenly become quite extraordinarily beautiful, and I saw that what she had to give, in every single respect, was exactly what I'd always wanted.

'Me neither,' I said, quite truthfully. 'We seem to find the same things funny, don't we?'

'We really do,' she said, and then: 'It's getting stuffy in here, isn't it? Have you got time for a bit of a walk? I could use some fresh air before I put my nose back to the grindstone.'

The hippie café was in the suburb of Clifton, which was a slightly more bohemian place then than it is now. We walked up to the green and then to the famous bridge across the Gorge. Neither of us had set a time limit on this little outing, but at about the point we paid our five pence toll and set out across the bridge, we must both have realised that we'd crossed some kind of line. But we pretended not to notice, continuing to talk animatedly about the course and our lives and the world in general as we headed, without actually discussing where we were going, towards the woods on the far side of the Gorge.

'I love Leigh Woods,' Nicola said, 'don't you? Have you got time to walk into them just a little bit?'

So then we were under the green leaves together, just me, and this dazzlingly beautiful grown-up who'd sought out my company, walking to a particular spot that Nicola knew, where we could stand and look down into the Gorge. The tide was in, I remember, and some sort of tugboat was coming up the river.

'I really meant what I said back there in the café, Rick. I didn't mean to be heavy about it, or to make you uncomfortable, and I'm really sorry if I embarrassed you, but I really do feel at home with you, like I've known you all my life.'

Soon after that, we kissed.

Looking back, she was quite controlling. She would readily cede power to me in bed or in conversation, as a parent cedes power to a child in play, but it was always her who set the boundaries. She was never free to see me in the evenings when her husband Derek was home, and usually had to head off in the middle of the afternoon to fetch her kids from school, but I had a bedsit not far from the campus, and we'd meet there for sex, sometimes in the morning, sometimes in the early afternoon, sometimes even in the one-hour gap between morning and afternoon lectures.

'I love Derek,' she told me, 'and I love my kids. When I finish the course here, we're moving to another city, and you and I will have to say goodbye. *Really* goodbye, I mean: no presents, no promises, no plans to meet again. But I want you to know that I've never loved anyone like I love you, and I never will for the rest of my life.'

Back in those days, when I got everywhere by walking, I had a little game that I used to play to keep me amused. I'd pick out some feature ahead of me, a lamp post perhaps, or a street corner, and try to imagine the me that would, in a few minutes, be walking past it. That person was a complete stranger to me, and indeed, while I was still walking towards my chosen point, he didn't even exist, wasn't even as substantial as a shadow. A couple of minutes later, when I reached the lamp post, or whatever landmark it was that I'd picked out, I'd look back at the spot where I'd been when I'd chosen it, and remember that past self from a few minutes ago. And of course it was *him* that was the stranger now, him that didn't exist. In fact, assuming that no one else had seen him, there wasn't a trace of him left in the world, outside of my own already fading and imperfect memory.

So I accepted Nicola's deal quite readily.

'The future doesn't matter,' I told her. 'What's important is that you're with me now.'

She *was* with me, she really was. Her body was solid, her lips were warm. I could feel her breath on my cheek. I could smell her sex on my hands and the warm scent on her neck, mingling with the aroma of her skin. I could hear her voice speaking just a few inches from my ear.

'I *am* with you now, my dearest, completely and utterly with you.'

We kissed and rolled about and laughed. There are times which are so complete and self-contained that it simply doesn't seem to matter whether or not they'll last. And a few minutes later, all that was real in the world was that I was pushing myself up inside her body, where I'd been so many times and would go again many times more. And Nicola was loudly welcoming me.

Never in my life until then had the world felt so rich and full and generous. Never mind the as-yet non-existent future; up to now even the living present had always felt remote and unattainable, as if I'd been condemned for some reason to eke out an existence outside the main flow of time, on some other meaner track that ran alongside it. And, if I'm to be completely honest, the only women I'd had an orgasm with up until then were not even three dimensional, but printed on glossy paper in magazines. I still remember the gluey smell of the ink.

'I love you, Nicola. I can't believe how much I love you. I didn't even know such a thing was even possible.'

'Nor did I, sweetheart,' she said, and I released myself inside her body.

I knew a lot about mythology back then – reading mythology is the kind of thing you do on that other meaner track – and now I told Nicola the famous story of how Tristan crossed the Irish Sea to fetch Iseult. He was to bring her back to Cornwall to marry his uncle, King Mark, and neither of them meant anything more to happen than that. But, passing the time together on the first evening, with no land in sight and no one to be with but one another, they accidentally drank a love potion. It hadn't been meant for the two of them. It was for Iseult and Mark, a gift sent from Ireland to bind together the newly married couple and ensure their happiness. But Iseult and Tristan took it for ordinary wine, drinking it down without a thought, and suddenly all that mattered to them was each other.

Of course, even back then in the days before history began, it wasn't that far from Ireland to Cornwall. Pretty soon the land appeared ahead of them: just a line on the horizon at first, and then hills, and cliffs, and settlements beside the water with tiny houses strewn on the slopes like little coloured dice. And then King Mark's castle came into view, with its battlements and its stern grey walls.

When there were only two weeks left before Nicola was to leave, the two of us still acted as if our time together would go on forever. But the parting loomed over us, and there was increasing hysteria in our refusal to think of anything other than now. And however hard we tried not to, we noticed clocks ticking, hands sweeping coldly round. Very soon we reached the final week, and the days began to rush by: six, five, four… It was like being in a car with no brakes and no steering, hurtling downhill. We could already see the lamp post straight ahead of us that we were going to crash into, and there was nothing we could do to avoid it.

Nicola had decided that, for our final meeting, we should cross the bridge again, and go back to that spot in the woods overlooking the Gorge, where the two of us had first kissed. When we reached it, she kissed me again, slowly and very gently, and then stepped back a little so she could look at my face.

'I think we should say goodbye now, Rick,' she said. 'Is that okay with you? When you're ready I'd like you to walk back over the bridge by yourself. I'll wait till you've had time to cross over, then follow after.'

I nodded. There had to be a moment, I could see that.

'I've brought you a little present,' she said.

'Oh Nicola, I haven't got you one. I thought you said no presents.'

'Don't worry, sweetheart, it's only a tiny thing, and no one but you will be able to tell that it's a present at all.'

She opened her hand and showed me a child's marble, a little larger than average, but in other respects perfectly ordinary, made of clear glass with a single twist of scarlet along its axis.

'I was tidying up after my kids,' she said, 'and I saw this lying on the floor. I thought it was a bit like what you and me will have from now on. A flame frozen in time, a flame captured forever at the very moment when it was burning brightest.'

We kissed one more time, much more slowly, holding each other tightly for a long time. Then I turned and walked back through the trees.

So now that glass marble was all I had left of her. Nicola had refused to tell me where she was going, and had always been quite clear that this would be the end, and that neither of us was ever to try and track the other down. Tracking people down was much harder, in any case, back in those days before the internet, and I didn't even know her married name, for she'd always used her maiden name on the course.

Over the weeks and months afterwards, I struggled to get through the absence that she'd left behind her, like I was some sort of jungle explorer trying to hack my way through a kind of inverted rain forest where everything was cold, and creepers clung to me with an icy grip whenever I tried to move. I remember going down to where we'd studied, just to see her name on the list of the students there, and remind myself that she was real. I remember visiting everywhere we'd been together: the woods, the place in Clifton, the café in the library where our friendship had begun. And I remember, many times a day, taking out that marble to feel it and look at it, reminding myself that Nicola had chosen it for me, Nicola had held it in her hand, Nicola had told me that it signified a love that would not die.

Of course, in my many long walks across the city, I'd already proved to myself again and again that the past wasn't even as substantial as a shadow. With my rational head I knew that my time with Nicola had no more substance now than the ghostly former selves I imagined when I looked back at the empty pools of lamplight behind me. But at the level of emotion,

I couldn't accept it. Perhaps it would have been easier if she hadn't been the first, and if the whole thing
hadn't taken place inside that bubble of secrecy
and finite time that had made it seem so much
brighter and more vivid than everyday life. Perhaps
it would have been better too if I hadn't imbibed
all those heroic stories of impossible doomed loves
like Tristan and Iseult's. But, for whatever reason,
I strained and strained against the great numb wall
of intervening space that separated me from her, not
knowing where she was, or who was now basking in
her lovely gentle smile, but determined not to admit
to myself that she'd gone.

I never got over that grief in the way that other
people around me seemed to do, ending love relationships, pushing through the sadness, and then
beginning new ones with the same optimism as
before. But I was a human being with needs and I
made pragmatic choices. I couldn't give up Nicola,
but I learnt to divide my heart into two compartments, and in that way, I was able to persuade both
myself and a woman called Julie that I was in love
with her. When we married, I regretted it almost at
once, and we were apart again in less than eight-
een months. I met another woman called Mary not
long afterwards, and in due course married again,
but after twelve unhappy and destructive years, that
ended too, this time very bitterly, with Mary demand-
ing that I leave, keeping the house and our two kids,

and making it as difficult as she could for me to see them at all.

I remember how I searched out that cold hard marble on the day I left them, taking it from a hiding place at the back of a drawer, and slipping it into my jacket pocket. I drove over to my parents' house, where I was going to stay until I'd found a place of my own. It was a longish journey, and I was exhausted by weeks of almost sleepless nights. Pausing for a rest in a layby, I took the marble from my pocket in the solitude of my car and turned it over in my hands, feeling its solidity and smoothness. Then, as I'd done many times before, I held it up to the window, so as to let the sunlight shine through that cold unmoving flame and make it look, if only very slightly, like something actually alive and burning.

'I still love you best, Nicola,' I whispered. 'Underneath everything else the fire's still there.'

But even I had to admit that this wasn't a fire that could actually *warm* me, so I divided my heart again, looked around me and eventually got together with another woman called Patrice, moving back to Bristol to be with her.

The thing with Patrice lasted for about a year and a half, until she made the decision that it was over. She didn't make a scene, or punish me as Mary had done, she simply informed me that she no longer wanted to be with me.

'I feel like I'm dealing with an automaton most of

the time,' she said. 'Some kind of robot that you've placed on Earth to represent you, while the real you goes off alone to somewhere deep inside yourself, where I can't possibly hope to follow.'

I knew she was right. She'd spotted the compartments in my heart: the small one I'd allowed her to enter, and the big one behind it with the padlocked door. And so, without even attempting to argue, I found myself a little flat and moved out.

This was a dark time. After so many failures, I'd lost all confidence in my ability either to love or to hold the love of others. But I still had the glass marble. I still had the frozen flame. It couldn't speak to me, or smile at me, or kiss me, it couldn't caress me or warm me in bed, but it still could, at least to some degree, reassure me. I *could* be loved, that was what the marble told me, and I was capable of love, for I had once loved and been loved most wonderfully.

One day I put the marble in my pocket and drove over to Clifton, looking for the café where Nicola had told me we were two of a kind. Of course, it had long since gone. Clifton was way too upmarket by then for sleepy little hippie businesses, and the café had been replaced by a shop selling hand-made fabrics. I'd planned to sit at our favourite table, but now I decided instead to recreate the walk to that place in the woods where Nicola and I had shared our first and last kisses. She wouldn't be with me, of course, but I persuaded myself that if I moved through that same space again, holding her present in my hand, it would bring her at least a little bit nearer.

Halfway across the bridge, though, I stopped. I don't know what had changed inside me, but I was suddenly appalled, almost to the point of nausea, by the idea of going over the same wretched ground, prodding that same old wound, and attempting yet one more time to construct the semblance of a living being out of absence and empty air. Clutching the marble tightly in my hand, I looked down into the drop. A wire mesh had been installed since my student days to prevent people throwing themselves off, as so many had done in the past, but there were small square holes cut in it, so as still to allow an uninterrupted view.

What did I remember of Nicola, I challenged myself? What did I *really* remember? I could call to mind, at least approximately, the colour of her hair and her eyes (brown in both cases, though her hair had likely faded by now, as my own had done). I could remember roughly how tall she was, and the fact that she was fairly slim. But now I tried, I couldn't call to mind even the vaguest image of her face, or hear in my head the sound of her voice. Yes, and apart from a few iconic words – 'You and me are two of a kind' – which had very possibly themselves been worn into new shapes by constant rehearsal, like buffeted pebbles in a stream, I couldn't clearly remember anything she'd said. All I could really be certain of was the fact that, at the time, I'd found her words engaging, and that she'd found my words engaging too. But that was a long time ago. I fancied myself to be a communist back then. I found Monty Python funny. I thought *On the Road* was the greatest work of literature I'd ever read. And Nicola, though I still thought of her as excitingly older than me, had been twenty years younger than I was now.

Wasn't it really the case that what I most loved Nicola for was simply her interest in me? Hadn't I loved her so very much because she was the first grown-up woman who'd treated me like a grown-up man, when I'd feared that might never happen at all? I remembered Nicola's friend Fay, that other mature student on the course. She'd been really strikingly beautiful, like a model or a film star, and I'd actually noticed her before I noticed Nicola, though she'd seemed so far out of my own league as not even to be worth fantasising about. But suppose Fay had sought me out to help her with her project, and suppose she'd been the one who'd leant towards me over a café table and told me that she and I were two of a kind. Was there really any doubt that I would have fallen for her just as I fell for Nicola?

After all, I didn't know who I was back then. Dear God, I didn't even experience myself as having a *face*! Wasn't it the truth that I'd have been happy to be told I was just like them by any halfway attractive human being, perhaps even men as well as women? And wouldn't I have been happy to believe it too?

I opened my hand and looked down at the marble. I'd been clutching it so tightly that it had made a small bruised dent in the flesh of my palm. Tears came to my eyes. I had invested so much in this little ball of glass. I had laboured so long and so hard to keep the cold flame burning.

But I reached out over the railing and let it fall.

Still Life

A small greenhouse stood on the paved backyard of a long unoccupied house. It had a concrete floor and a single aluminium shelf. On the shelf stood three empty plastic flowerpots, with a fourth lying on its side. A watering can, moulded from red plastic, rested on the floor by the door.

It was the middle of a summer afternoon. Up until midday, the sky had been clear. All morning, the radiation had been pouring down from the sun, with no cloud in the way to reflect it back. Outside the greenhouse, the sun had warmed the soil and the roof of the house, and heated the black tarmac of the road it stood on to the point that it had become soft and sticky. In their turn, the soil, the road and the roof had warmed the air above them. As the air warmed, it had risen upwards, cooler air flowing in beneath it to take its place.

Inside the greenhouse the sun had also heated everything that was there: the aluminium, the concrete, the plastic pots and the red watering can. They too had warmed the air above them, but, unlike the air outside, the air in the greenhouse was trapped by the glass roof, which meant that, even when it was hot, it still remained close to the warm concrete and the aluminium and the plastic. And so the concrete and the metal and the plastic had continued to heat the same already-heated air, as if they were a hot-plate on a stove, and the greenhouse was a saucepan with its lid on. The air became very hot in there, and far hotter than the air outside.

Later on, as morning turned to afternoon, the sky clouded over and a cold wind began to blow. The air outside the greenhouse, already so much cooler than the air within, became colder still. But the air *in* the greenhouse, still sitting over that warm concrete and aluminium, stayed warm. It would cool down eventually, of course, but it would do so much more slowly than the air outside. Only the glass cooled quickly, because of the cold air rushing over it.

It so happened that the humidity was high that day. Inside the greenhouse, the warm air came up against the much colder glass, and some of the water vapour that it was carrying began to condense on the cool surface. Quite soon, the whole inner surface of the glass was steamed up, covered in a layer of tiny water droplets.

Some of these water droplets were heavier than the others, to the point where the constant tugging of the planet Earth beneath them became stronger than the surface tension that held them against the glass. The droplets on the glass windows began to slip downwards and, as they slipped, they collided with other droplets, absorbing the water into themselves and so becoming heavier still. The larger they grew, the smaller was their surface area in relation to their mass. As a result, the pull of the planet became stronger, relatively speaking, and the surface tension weaker. So the drops moved more quickly, and absorbed water more quickly too from yet more droplets. And all the greenhouse's windows were striped with the paths that these heavy drops had made.

The same thing happened under the glass roof, but here, when they had accumulated enough mass, the droplets didn't just slide down the inside of the glass but also began to drip. The drips fell straight downwards through the still-warm air inside the greenhouse, to splash onto the concrete floor, or the aluminium shelf, or sometimes onto the plastic pots or the can.

Having shed some of its weight in this way, a droplet would stop dripping, its surface tension once again strong enough to hold it together, and it would resume its descent down the inside slope of the roof, until it had accumulated enough water from smaller drops to rupture once more and release drips.

This sequence of events had happened many times. One of its consequences was that, while the glass of the roof, like that of the windows, was striped with the trails of water droplets, these roof trails were punctuated at more or less regular intervals with bulges, like beads on a necklace, where the water had paused and dripped.

And so, although the glass inside the greenhouse had been dry in the middle of the morning, now there were stripes of water on the walls, beads of water on the ceiling, and drips of water falling at regular intervals from the ceiling to the floor.

People were not involved in this story. There were no human beings present at all. There was *life* in the vicinity, it was true: weeds grew just outside the greenhouse – nettles, speedwell, grass, dandelions – and among this vegetation there lived earwigs, spiders, slugs, woodlice and snails. But none of them had anything at all to do with the stripes, or the beads, or the steady drips.

The only actors here were air, water vapour, sunlight, glass and gravity. And though all of these are more or less smooth and continuous things, the interaction between them had nevertheless produced rhythm and form.

Beyond the glass of the greenhouse roof, and far above it, new dark clouds were moving rapidly through the atmosphere.

They were also made of drops of water, and these water droplets were clumping together up there in the clouds, like the droplets had done inside the greenhouse.

And presently fat drops began to fall from them, spinning and turning through all that empty air, until they splashed on the greenhouse roof, ran down its glass, and trickled off it again in tiny water-falls, onto the weeds and the soil.

Dear

A man called James lives in one of the two ground-floor bedsits. He's the same sort of age as me, in his early thirties. He is tolerably good looking, always wears a jacket and tie and is, as my aunt Angelica puts it, 'very well spoken', all of which would also be a fair description of myself. I first met him when Angelica became convinced that some intruder was 'prowling round' inside the building. At her request, I called on every resident to ask if they'd seen strangers on the stairs.

When James met me at his door, I could see him noticing my surprise that a man like him should be living in a place like this. The two of us really were quite alike, and he acknowledged this with an odd little smile: sly, complicit, and strangely self-satisfied.

'By the way,' he told me, when we'd finished discussing Angelica's imaginary prowlers, 'I should warn you that I may not remember you if I see you again. Did a stupid thing, you see, a few years back. Got a bit depressed and tried to kill myself with the exhaust of my car. I wouldn't recommend it. Memory's all shot to pieces. Can't hold onto anything for more than ten minutes or so.'

It seemed odd to me that he should reveal something so personal when we'd only just met, but the strangest part was the way he smiled as he told me about his calamity. It was the same smile he'd greeted me with, the smile of a schoolboy with a sick note that will get him off for the rest of term.

On the opposite side of the hall to James lives a Brummie woman called Sheila, who James refers to as 'the bag lady'. I gather she's in her fifties, though it would be hard to tell, because she has no front teeth, a ravished, bloodshot face, and is sort of shapeless, as if all the various parts of her body have been broken up so many times that, in the end, any attempt to properly reassemble them has been abandoned, and they've just been tossed anyhow into a roughly body-shaped sack. According to James, who seems to know a surprising amount for a man with a ten-minute memory, she really did used to live on the streets until Dr Hodgson took her in. 'She still drinks a bottle of sherry a day,' he told me, smiling as he watched my eyes for a reaction.

Sheila dotes on James, cleans his room and brings him cups of tea. I've had to call in on him a number of times since that first occasion, all in connection with various worries of my aunt's, and I've several times witnessed him receiving these offerings of Sheila's in a way that reminds me of some colonial district officer accepting a gift from a benighted native: amused, puzzled, slightly contemptuous, but nevertheless pleased. 'I know it's absurd, but what can I do about it?' his half-apologetic expression seems to say as he glances towards me and sees me watching. But it is only *half*-apologetic. There's always that trace of self-satisfaction and complicity. He and I are too well brought up to mention it, that look seems to say, but we both know I secretly envy him for living in a bedsit with a worn lino floor, and having a bag lady to care for him.

Once, on some errand of my aunt's, I intruded on the two of them watching a TV game show. James was in his armchair, Sheila kneeling at his feet with her hand inside his fly.

'Oops,' he said, pushing her away. 'Bad moment.'

But even then, he smiled.

On the next floor lives a man named Doug. He's now in his fifties, like Sheila, but I gather he spent most of his early life in some kind of institution, a hospital for the mentally retarded or some such thing, from which he was discharged in his twenties into what is called The Community. Even after thirty years, he still misses that place. He's told me many times that he used to work in the laundry there, and the highlight of his day was riding round on the back of an electric vehicle from ward to ward, picking up sacks of dirty clothes, and dropping off clean ones. Everyone knew him, he says. Staff and patients, high grades and low grades: everyone in the whole hospital knew Doug the laundryman.

Perhaps surprisingly, in view of his laundry experience, Doug doesn't go in for washing things. Every time I see him, he's wearing the same black suit which has become shiny with the particles of grease that now fill in each gap between one fibre and the next. The flat stinks of cigarette smoke, old chip fat, urine and sour stale sweat.

Doug's not much good with money either. From what he tells me, he pawns his wristwatch for a few quid at the end of most weeks and then buys it back again for twice as much when his benefits come through. Sometimes, when I call on him, he asks me for a loan: 'just a couple of quid, mate, to tide me over till Friday'. I never get the money back, but that doesn't stop him, a week or two later, making the same request without so much as a mention of the existing debt.

Next to Doug is a bedsit which Dr Hodgson – the Doctor, as his tenants call him – keeps for his own use on his visits to Bristol. He was born in the city and used to live and work here, but these days he's a reader in mathematics at the University of Edinburgh. At first glance, he's quite imposing to look at – well over six feet tall, strong, broad-shouldered and boyishly handsome for a man in his early sixties – but at second glance you see that the man himself barely inhabits this body. It's like a suit of clothes that's several sizes too big for him, and way too flashy. Someone much smaller and more diffident peeps out of its eyes, someone more like his own tenants, and more like me.

He's a considerate landlord. He doesn't keep the house in brilliant repair, but this is down to his unworldliness, rather than meanness or indifference to the well-being of the residents. He always gets problems fixed as soon as they're raised with him without a quibble, and his rents are extremely low.

My aunt Angelica has the whole top floor to herself, so that her place isn't a bedsit like the others but a proper flat, with a bedroom, living room, small kitchen and even a tiny spare room. She became quite friendly with the Doctor for a while, about a decade ago, at a time when he was based in Oxford for a year and came over to Bristol pretty much every weekend. The two of them had tea together a few times, apparently, and on one occasion – one fateful occasion – she even cooked him a meal.

Now Angelica stares at me with her enormous eyes. Her cup of tea has come to a standstill halfway to her mouth.

'He's visiting again?'

'That's right, Aunty. He phoned me to let me know.'

I replace my own slightly grubby teacup on its chipped saucer.

'This is his house, after all,' I point out. 'He is entitled to come.'

I live about two miles away and visit every couple of days. It's a duty I perform at the request of my mother, Angelica's younger sister. ('I'm so sorry to put this onto you, David, but I really need you to do it for me. Angelica needs a lot of support, but for all kinds of reasons to do with our childhood relationship – don't worry, darling, I won't bore you with it now! – I'm just not up to taking it on.')

'He might be entitled to come here in a legal sense,' Aunt Angelica says. 'But that's entirely beside the point. *Why* does he need to come, that's what I want to know?'

As in the rest of the building, there's a faint whiff of decay in Angelica's flat. She adds considerably to the general dinginess by keeping the curtains drawn and the windows firmly closed, but it's all very genteel. There's a three-piece suite in a slightly threadbare floral print, a dresser with a dinner set on display, and a china shepherdess on the mantelpiece above the small gas fire.

'He must know how much it upsets me,' she says. 'And it unsettles the others too, particularly that poor old Doug who of course he should never have taken on in the first place.'

Angelica sees herself, among other things, as Doug's protector. He comes up to her flat quite often, and she meets him at her door to dispense handfuls of coins as grandly as if she was the lady of the manor and he was some kind of grateful peasant. But as far as I've been able to gather, neither Doug nor the other two tenants are troubled in any way by their landlord's visits. Quite the contrary,

in fact: James enjoys the contact with another edu-
cated man, Sheila thinks he's 'lovely' and 'a perfect
gent', and, perhaps because of his institutional
background, Doug is quite obsessed with him, to
the point where much of his conversation seems to
revolve around what the Doctor said last time, what
he said in reply, and what he's going to say to the
Doctor when he visits next. None of this, however, is
of any interest to Angelica.

'There's no real reason for him to come,' she
insists. 'It's not as if he works in this town any more.'

Like her eyes, her mouth is very large in comparison to her tiny face and frame and is tremendously
expressive in an almost cartoon-like way.

'And in any case,' she adds quickly, before I can
point out that in fact he does still have academic
commitments down here, even if he is based in Scotland, 'there are such things as hotels, and the man
is absolutely made of money. I really don't see why
I should endure this, year after year after year!'

Anxiety eats at her constantly, and almost literally so, for it's anxiety that burns up the calories and
makes her so painfully thin. But Aunt Angelica is
much too proud to ever speak of fear, and so she
talks instead about irritation and displeasure, about
feelings trampled, and rights infringed.

'You don't have to see him, though, Aunty,' I
point out. 'He'll stay downstairs. He won't call on
you. Remember we agreed that with him? He won't
disturb you in any way.'

My aunt lowers her cup, her large eyes bright, her large lips curling in patrician scorn.

'He won't call on me, you say? Oh really, is that so? Honestly, David, how can I be expected to believe that, in view of the history? Have you forgotten that he once came right up here – right up! – expecting to be invited in?'

'Yes he did, but that was five years ago. And I spoke to him afterwards, if you remember. I explained to him that you didn't like it, and that you wanted to be left alone. If you recall, he was very apologetic. He told me that he was just trying to be friendly, as he is with his other three tenants, and he hadn't understood how you felt. And, as you know, he promised faithfully he'd never do it again.'

'"Oh Angelica! Angelica!"' Angelica distorts her whole face as she mocks Dr Hodgson's soft voice, making it sound not just mild and tentative, as it certainly is in reality, but weak and wheedling too. '"I wondered if I might pop in for a chat?" And it was three years ago, anyway. Get your facts right, David. Three years, nine months and twenty days, to be exact.'

'Okay, three years then, Aunt Angelica. That's still a long time. And that was all he said. He didn't come into the flat. He didn't ask anything of you. And when you told him to go, he went. It's just that he owns the house, and he thought it was a shame that you and he couldn't be on friendly terms as you used to be. It's not as if—'

'It's not as if what? It's not as if he ever returned my feelings? Is that what you're going to say? That it was all in my head? Ha! Some chance, David! Some chance! By all means believe that if it makes you happy, but he and I both know that's a lie, even if he's not man enough to admit it! That man was positively slavering over me, David, positively slavering! But he's had his chance, and he's not getting another.'

Angelica laughs grimly.

'And then of course there was that time I heard him shouting. Do you remember? Shouting and crying down there, late at night, all by himself.'

'He apologised for that too, if you remember. You asked me to speak to him and he apologised. He's only human, Aunt Angelica. Life is hard for him as it is for most of us. He was upset with himself about something and he started shouting. It wasn't aimed at you. It was about something else entirely.'

'Or so he says, anyway. Or so he says. I'm not quite so trusting as you are, David, I'm afraid. Not so trusting at all. But who cares anyway? I don't want him here, and there's an end to it. If he's really got business in this town, which I very much doubt, why can't he just stay in a hotel?'

'But like I keep saying, it's his house. If you really don't want anything to do with him, you could move somewhere else yourself, but you've always—'

'You're always nagging me to move, aren't you? Somewhere cheaper, perhaps, is that the idea? So I won't use up your inheritance?'

This is a preposterous charge. There's absolutely no chance of her finding anything cheaper than her present flat, whose rent hasn't increased for a decade, but there's no point in my saying that, so I keep quiet.

'This may be his house,' Angelica adds, 'but it's my home.' She must know that the thing about my inheritance is nonsense. She has very little money, and will have none before she's through. 'Why should I move out because of him?'

When I next visit, Angelica is fretful.

'When will he arrive? You must tell me, David. I must know in advance, so I can be quite sure I won't have anything whatever to do with him.'

She gives a characteristic sniff, contemptuous and haughty. My aunt seldom ventures beyond the door of her flat, but she acts like the queen of the world.

'Not that I won't know anyway,' she adds. 'You are your mother's son, David, completely rhinoceros-skinned, and you don't have my sensitivity at all. But I can *feel* things, and I *always* sense his presence through the floor. The weight of him plodding around, and those big slow clunky thoughts going round and round in his head!'

'Listen, Angelica. Listen. You mustn't distress yourself, but he—'

'He's what? He's *what*? Oh dear God, David, you're not telling me he's here *already*?'

'Yes, he arrived when—'

'He's here and you didn't tell me! How *could* you! How could—'

She breaks off. She is *so* transparent. It's just occurred to her that, if she admits to not knowing he's here already, she'll be undermining her own claim to be able to detect his presence and sense his thoughts.

'Yes, of course, of course,' she says crossly. 'I can feel him down there now. That heaviness. Those heavy thoughts going round and round and leading nowhere. I noticed them earlier. But you'd specifically promised me that you'd tell me in advance and so I'd persuaded myself I must be wrong.'

She's very agitated now and gets up to fetch her cigarettes from the dresser, fumbling one out of the packet, lighting it, drawing deeply and then laying it down in the glass ashtray that always sits beside her on its slightly grubby doily. Almost straight away she begins to take another cigarette out of the packet, and then remembers the first one. Another person might be amused by her own absent-minded mistake, but Angelica never laughs at herself. She pushes the second cigarette back into the pack, and tosses it crossly down.

'He arrived in the early hours,' I tell her. 'You were probably still asleep. He won't disturb you, and very soon he'll go out.'

'What time will he go out? I must know what time. And the time he's coming back as well. I often look out of the window, you know. Often. It's my view, my peaceful view, and he's no right to spoil it by making me worry that I might see him there.'

I look out of Angelica's window myself sometimes, when I find myself alone in the living room – it *is* a lovely view, and I always admire those rows of blue slate roofs, climbing the hillside opposite – but I've never once seen my aunt look out for the pleasure of it. The only occasions I've ever observed her pull back the curtains is when she hears some noise in the street below, some potential threat. She has no resources spare for mere curiosity. She is in a permanent state of emergency. Everything is in the service of defence.

'I've already got the times,' I tell her.

Knowing how she'd fuss, I spoke to him earlier on the phone. It was extremely embarrassing, asking my aunt's landlord to spell out the precise times when he would leave and return to his own house, but of course he was as gentle as ever.

'I'm *so* sorry that Angelica and I have had this misunderstanding, David. It seems to cause her so much distress. I really do assure you that I only ever intended to offer her my friendship, but in my clumsy way, I somehow gave her the wrong impression. And then, when I tried to put her straight, I got *that* wrong as well. I really am *so* sorry. I'd ask you to pass on my apologies but, from what you tell me, that would only upset the situation even more.'

'And he mustn't look up,' Angelica adds. 'When he comes in and goes out he must *not*

look up! Do you understand? David, answer me!
Do – you – under*stand*?'

Why do I put up with this? Why do I keep coming
here to be bullied by my mother's mad sister, who
never asks me a single thing about myself, and never
wonders, even for a moment, whether I might have
worries or troubles of my own? Am I really doing
this out of altruism and family feeling, or am I just
submitting to her power?

For she *is* powerful, that's the strange thing.
Angelica is so utterly terrified of the world that she
doesn't leave her flat for months on end. And yet,
somehow, she still wields enormous power. 'I'll tell
him, Aunt Angelica. As to those times you asked for:
he'll be going out at—'

'I don't even like *you* speaking to him, you know.
It really isn't very nice for me having to talk to you
when I know you've spoken to him earlier in the day.
In fact, to be frank with you, David, I'm surprised
that didn't occur to you.'

I'm really cross now. 'Well, what *do* you want me
to do, Aunty? I need to speak to him, don't I, if you
want me to find out about his movements?'

She's noticed the sharpness in my voice and,
just for a moment, I can see her considering it. But
then she hears some sound – she's very sensitive
to sound – and imperiously holds her hand up for
silence.

'What was that?'

'Just a toilet flushing, Aunty.'

'Just a toilet flushing, you say. Do toilets flush themselves, then, David? It was *him* flushing it, you mean. Him. Did you think you could leave out that obvious fact?'

'*Him* flushing it, then.' Once again I can't quite keep the irritation from my voice. 'But now it's quiet.'

My aunt glances at my face. She has certainly registered my annoyance, but she's not planning to flatter it with her attention, for if there's one single thing in the world she's not afraid of, it's me. She sniffs.

'I notice you *still* haven't told me when he's going out and coming back.'

'He'll go out at nine thirty and return just after five.'

'He mustn't come back any earlier then. He's told you his plans, and now he must stick to them. If he finishes his business sooner than expected, he'll just have to sit and wait in the park. His *so-called* business, I should really say, because I'm not fooled, David, even if you are. I know perfectly well that he just comes here because of me. It's utterly pathetic, but it seems that's how he gets his little kicks.'

'I really don't think it is, Aunt Angelica. You're not quite such a big figure in his mind as he is in—'

'Not back before five. You must make him promise that.'

Angelica is waiting. She's beside the window, hiding behind the curtain but peeking out. It's 4.30 in the afternoon.

'What are *you* doing here at this hour?' she demands, dropping the curtain immediately and stepping back with a flounce. 'I sometimes wonder what they pay you for, David, in that job of yours. Don't you have *work* to do?'

'I thought I'd check if you were alright.'

'Well, obviously I'm not. How *could* I be alright, when he's on his way back here? He'll probably be early. I know his timekeeping of old. So I was just having one last look at my lovely peaceful view before he spoiled it.'

'Those blue roofs, eh? Those blue roofs climbing up the hill?'

'Yes. But why do you say it in that sarcastic way? I must say you've been *very* unpleasant and sarcastic lately, David. I don't know why you're out of sorts, but I don't think it's very grown-up or fair of you to take it out on me.' She snorts. 'I suppose you were trying to hint that I was looking out for *him*, were you? *Some* chance! He should be so lucky. *He – should – be – so – lucky.*'

She crosses the room, picks up her cigarettes, fumbles the lighter open with her shaky hands.

'Well, alright,' she says. 'I *was* looking out for him. But only to check that he kept his promise. Only for that.'

My tiny aunt pulls deeply at her cigarette, exhales, then glares defiantly out at me with her enormous eyes from the middle of a poisonous white cloud.

•

Angelica is listening.

She is *really* listening. She's standing quite motionless in the middle of the room, her head tipped over to the right, her right ear positively straining towards the floor. She even holds back a wisp of her featherlight hair so as not to obstruct her hearing in any way.

'He talks to himself, you know. I can hear him talking all the time. "*Mumble, mumble, mumble,*" he goes. "*Angelica this, Angelica that, Angelica three bags full.*"'

She stands up straight. She lets that little wisp of hair fall back over her ear. She looks for her cigarettes.

'You think I make it all up, don't you? You really are *so* like your mother.' She shrugs, lights a cigarette, draws deeply on it. 'Well, you can believe what you like, David. It's entirely up to you. But he *does* talk about me. Of course he does. How could he avoid it, when he thinks about me all the time?'

'I'm sure he does think about you. I'm sure he really does care about you, as he cares for all the people in this building. And in your case, he remembers how it was, before… well, before you developed these *feelings* for him, when the two of you could just be friends. He wishes things could be like that again.'

'He puts it all onto me, does he? How *very* convenient.'

'He'd like to see you. He told me so himself. In fact he said he'd *love* to see you if—'

'That's *enough*! That's more than enough. You

promised me – you *promised* me, David – that you wouldn't pass on a single word he said.'

She cocks her head, pulls back her wisp of hair, listening once more with all her might. Then, apparently hearing nothing new, she stands up straight.

'He had a visitor yesterday evening. I couldn't tell who it was.'

She takes another long draw on her cigarette, looking over at me all the while in a sideways, sneaky sort of way.

'And you are *certainly* not going to tell me, are you, David? That would be *quite* against all those high principles of yours.'

Getting no reply from me, she cocks her head again, and listens to the floor for a few seconds more before giving an irritated shrug and stubbing out the cigarette. I don't know anyone who can consume a cigarette as fast as my aunt Angelica.

'Typical of him, really. "I know what I'll do," he says to himself, "I'll invite a mystery guest. *That* will arouse Angelica's interest! *That* will get her going!" Well, let me tell you this, David, I'm not the *slightest* bit interested. Not the slightest. Some floozy no doubt, some little tart. What concern is that of mine? In fact, even if you *did* try to tell me who the visitor was, I wouldn't listen. Certainly not. I'd block my ears and make a sound like this.'

She sticks her fingers in her ears, and chants 'Na na na na na!'

•

Angelica is angry.

'Why didn't you say he was about to go?'

She is pacing around her room, smoking furiously. Her face is pale and taut.

'When was it anyway? Last night? Oh I *knew* it! I just knew it! I heard the door as he crept out. He tried to do it quietly of course, the coward, but he's always been a clumsy oaf. And then I heard a car starting up, down towards the end of the street. I suppose he thought I wouldn't know it was him if he parked right down there at the bottom, but I knew alright. I knew it was his car. I heard it pause at the turning and then move off again. And then afterwards I heard the silence. No thoughts down there any more from beneath my floor. No mumbling and muttering and thumping about. Just silence once again.'

She glares at me.

'Don't smirk at me in that knowing way, David. You look just like your mother. I heard all of that, all of it, whether you believe me or not. But you hadn't *told* me, had you? You'd let me down yet *again*. You'd absolutely promised you'd tell me, and yet you said nothing. And so naturally I doubted myself.'

She turns and hurries through to the little kitchen at the back of the flat, running, almost, in her eagerness. Pulling back the curtain, she presses her face against the window to peer down at the tiny back yard, with its empty washing line and its concrete slabs and its five metal dustbins in a row, with the flat numbers marked in yellow paint: 27A, 27B, 27C, 27D, 27E.

She turns back into the room.

'All night I listened to the car. I heard it going through the streets, and then up the motorway. Birmingham, the North, Scotland, up and up and up. All those lonely places in the night. All those cold orange lights shining down... I knew he'd gone but you hadn't told me so I thought perhaps I was going mad. *You – should— have – told – me!*'

'He had to leave earlier than he thought. He'll probably be back again next year, but—'

'It's entirely up to him, David. Why should I care? What difference does it make to me?'

She turns once again to the kitchen window, looks down at the bins. Those blue roofs wind unnoticed over the hill.

'I expect he's left all kinds of rubbish down there.'

'I shouldn't have thought so. He's only been here a day. What sort of rubbish did you have in mind?'

Angelica snorts.

'All kinds of rubbish,' she repeats firmly. 'He always does, the great lout. He leaves a trail of the stuff wherever he goes.'

When I go back later in the day, I find Angelica outside.

She almost *never* ventures down the stairs – a van delivers her shopping and the man carries the bags up to her – but now she's come down, and out through the front door, and into the great terrifying space under the sky. As I arrive, she's making her way round the back of the house, using her left hand to maintain contact with the building's reassuring wall, and keeping up a constant muttered monologue to hold the world at bay. She hasn't noticed that I'm here.

'All kinds of rubbish,' she says to herself, with that haughty little snort of a laugh and, though she herself lives in Flat E, she heads straight for the bin marked 27D.

'Aha!' she mutters as she lifts the lid. 'I knew it.'

At the bottom of the bin she's seen a small plastic bag, such as might line a wastepaper basket. She still hasn't noticed me as she reaches in, with a grunt of effort and pulls out the bag, emptying its contents onto the ground. There's an apple core, a free newspaper, a box that once contained a ready-cooked beef lasagne, and the soiled metal tray in which the lasagne was cooked. But what interests her is a little scrumpled ball of blue paper. It looks like a discarded letter, or a draft found wanting and thrown away. One corner is stained brown by the lasagne.

Angelica kneels on the ground to smooth it out against the concrete. Yesterday's date is scrawled at the top and after that...

But I can't watch this in silence any more.

'Aunty Angelica?' I murmur.

Still on her knees, she wheels round like some small cornered animal.

'What are *you* doing here?' she hisses, clutching

the crumpled paper against herself as she clambers hastily to her feet. 'I really can't *stand* the way you keep creeping and snooping round me. *So* like your mother. I'm a grown-up woman, for goodness sake, David. Do you really think I can't look after myself?'

'Well, sometimes you do need a bit of help, Aunty, and you did seem very upset earlier. I was just calling by to make sure you were alright, and then I noticed you down here by the bins.'

'So you thought you'd have a bit of a laugh at old Angelica, did you? Have a bit of a laugh, eh, and then get in your mother's good books by telling her the whole story? Go away, David. I don't want you. Just go, go, go!'

But a few hours later, she calls me in tears, begging me to come back over.

I let myself into the flat with my own key and find her sobbing on the floor beside her dresser. She's still clinging to that little piece of paper, though she's scrumpled it back up into a sodden ball. Gently I remove it from her hand and set it down.

Some time later, when I've poured her a brandy and tucked her up for the night, I have a look at it, but there's almost nothing to see. All that's written there, apart from the date, is the single word which most letters begin with.

I meet James on my way out. He's coming back from the shops with a few purchases in a carrier bag.

'Good evening,' he says blandly – whatever the truth about his memory, he recognises me perfectly well every time he sees me – and then he gives me that smile.

There is poor David, that smile seems to say. There is David with all his responsibilities and pressures and painful attachments. There is David the ever-anxious juggler, still trying desperately to keep those clubs in the air. And here, on the other hand, is lucky James, with his life-long sick note, giving him permission to let them fall.

Rage

On that particular morning I'd travelled down to London by train from Cambridge, where I'd been participating in a conference on problems of governance in emerging economies, and had stayed overnight with some friends. I arrived at King's Cross at 8.15 or thereabouts. I stood in a queue at a food stall for a couple of minutes, meaning to buy myself a croissant and a cappuccino, then decided that I really didn't need them. I'd already had one breakfast and I was, and still am, over two stone overweight. So I abandoned the queue and headed down to the southbound Piccadilly Line in order to travel to the Holborn offices of a certain NGO, small, but highly regarded in the field, which funds experimental agricultural projects in southern Africa. They'd commissioned me and an old colleague of mine called Emily to do an evaluation of one of their projects, and we were due to present our provisional findings at 9.30.

There was a train waiting at the platform. I climbed onto it near the front and, although of course it was pretty full at that time of the morning, I was lucky enough to find myself a seat. On the way up from Cambridge, I'd gone over our provisional report and jotted down some key points. Now, as the train moved off, I went back over the notes I'd written to make sure I'd got them clear in my mind. I was keen to make a good impression because I wanted to pick up more commissions from this particular outfit. They paid well and I needed the work. My wife and I had recently separated, so we had two houses to pay for instead of one, and my daughter Jasmine was about to start at university.

The doors closed. The train picked up speed and plunged into the southbound tunnel. I looked up for a moment at my travelling companions: Londoners – black, white, brown – reading, playing with their phones, listening to music, or just quietly sitting or standing in that little capsule of air and electric light and thinking their private thoughts as they hurtled through concrete and clay. People sometimes talk about the loneliness and alienation of big cities but I felt a surge of affection for these city folk, who every single day encounter many times more human beings than they could hope to get to know in an entire lifetime. How many other species would sit quietly and harmoniously in such a confined space with so many fellow creatures they'd never met?

I arrived at the office in time to get a cup of coffee before the meeting, and have a quick word with Emily, who'd travelled up from Brighton. Two more people arrived, Peter and Amina – we knew both of them pretty well: the overseas development community is a small world – and the four of us went through into the meeting room to wait for the most important person, Sue, who as head of the NGO's research section, had commissioned our work.

Sue arrived late, looking very agitated.

'Haven't you heard the news? There's been a whole series of bomb attacks in the Underground. The whole tube system has shut down.'

We put off the start of the meeting. Amina set up her laptop on the table so we could watch the unfolding story, both to figure out its immediate implications for our day and to process it in a more general sense. There were suggestions at first that as many as six bombs had gone off, but the reports gradually settled on three: three different trains, one at Aldgate, one at Edgware Road and one at Russell Square. But then, just when that seemed to have been clarified, another bomb went off on a bus. How many more would there be?

I don't remember the timing of it all, but at some point I figured out that the train bombed at Russell Square was on the southbound Piccadilly Line and must have followed directly after the one I travelled on. I looked back at my peaceful space capsule, hurtling through the earth, and imagined another one just like it, another collection of ordinary London people – white, black, brown – reading, listening to music, or just thinking their own thoughts, as they followed my train into that same dark tunnel. But,

in their case, this familiar scene had been abruptly
torn away like some flimsy canvas backdrop. Some
of them would have been buried under corpses, or
trapped by bits of train, or impaled by other people's bones. Some would have been blown to pieces.
Some would just be terrified. I imagined a second
or two of silence and then screaming voices everywhere, from up and down the train, like the voices
of the damned in hell.

'My feeble attempt at dieting hasn't succeeded in
reducing my weight,' I told the others, my voice wobbly, 'but it may quite possibly have saved my life. If
I'd bought that croissant, I'd have missed the train I
came on, and caught the one after.'

I was pretty shaken for many days afterwards, but
I didn't suffer the survivor guilt that some people
report after a close shave of that kind. I guess one
day I may eat these words, but I've never really *got*
that 'Why me?' stuff. The answer, it seems to me, is
quite simple: I didn't buy the croissant. What more
do people expect? How exactly do they imagine this
universe is arranged?

And as to the question of why anyone could feel
justified in killing and maiming people who he or
she didn't even know, well, that wasn't a mystery to
me either.

Nowadays, when white British folk like me hear the
word *terrorist* we think of some fanatical Islamist
dreaming of martyrdom and paradise, his beliefs

utterly alien to our own. My neighbour George, for instance, is a philosophy lecturer who is irritated to distraction by anything that isn't logical, and he blames the whole phenomenon, firstly on the backwardness of the Islamic religion, and secondly, and more generally, on religion itself. If only these people could be weaned off their medieval belief in a superior being and persuaded to embrace secular, scientific, progressive modernity, then, in George's view, this irrational and ugly behaviour would cease.

But George is very young, and I've reached the age when even philosophers look like kids. I remember the terrorists of the sixties and seventies: the Baader-Meinhof gang in Germany, the Red Brigades in Italy, the Popular Front for the Liberation of Palestine, the Basques and the IRA. None of them were motivated by religion, and most of them, including even the Arabs, were Marxists: which is to say that they subscribed to an ideology that saw itself *precisely* as secular, scientific and progressive. What's more, the European terrorists often came from very similar backgrounds to my neighbour George and myself. Andreas Baader and Ulrike Meinhof, for instance, both came from middle class academic families, just like the family I grew up in, or George's family now.

So, yes, in these present times, it is young Muslims who are being drawn to the possibilities of random murder as a way of making a political or moral point. But in my teenage years that particular pressure wave was passing through a different medium, and was much closer to my own world and my own experience. And, sequestered though I was in the bubble-like environment of a private boarding school, I myself felt its pull.

I fancied myself as a writer back then and I remember writing a story when I was fifteen or so, which contrasted two figures. One of them was a kind of Christian guru, a bit like Mother Teresa, to whom the famous and powerful came for spiritual guidance; the other was a greasy-haired loner who built bombs in his mouldy bedsit and threw them randomly into crowds. The point of the story was that it was the terrorist who was the truly good person, even though he had a crappy personality and everyone hated him. The guru bolstered an unjust world by making the powerful feel good, but the terrorist, by making everyone feel bad, was driving the world towards change.

The school was called Shotsford House and its main building was a former stately home, surrounded by woodland and chalky hills. It saw itself as progressive – no fagging, for instance, no cane and no cold showers, though these were all still common at that time – and it had a sort of Christian humanist ethos of a kind that was more widespread in those days than it is now.

Here, for instance, is the headmaster, standing at his podium at morning assembly. His name is Mr

Frobisher. 'Blessed are the poor in spirit,' he booms out, 'for theirs is the Kingdom of Heaven.' He pauses for several seconds, his great head bowed over the book, wind whistling in and out of his nostrils. *Christ*, that man could ham it up! Then suddenly he looks up at us with fiery and accusing eyes. 'Blessed are the *poor – in – spirit*,' he repeats, and begins to speak with passionate intensity of the selfishness, greed and crass materialism of the modern world. 'Grab what you can,' he hisses, clawing at the air, his whole face distorted by the ugliness he wants to convey. 'Grab what you can by whatever means you can get away with, and to *hell* with everyone else.' The country is in the middle of a railway strike – large industrial strikes were pretty frequent occurrences back then – and Mr Frobisher uses this as an illustration of his point. The railwaymen, he says, are 'opportunists of the worst kind, holding the whole community to ransom, *not* for the sake of some great cause, but for *colour television sets* and *bigger cars*.' He almost spits out the words.

Now comes the pause again, the bowing of the head, the whistling wind. 'You are very privileged,' he concludes in a new soft voice. 'You will have many opportunities. You could very easily use those opportunities for purely personal gain. But I beg you, I beg all of you, to make them into opportunities to serve.'

After another silence, he lifts his head, and becomes suddenly brisk and business-like as he turns to the more mundane everyday business, of which we all of us must take our share. He makes various announcements. And finally he issues one of his regular reminders that 'decorum and courtesy' are expected at all times when potential pupils are being shown round the school with their parents.

These people might arrive in brand new Jaguars, the tense-faced little boys in the uniforms of expensive preparatory schools, the mothers in furs, the fathers with heavy Rolexes on their wrists, but *their* crass materialism will never in any circumstances be pointed out.

I planned a terror attack with my best friend Jules. We'd recently seen the Lindsay Anderson film *if...* and it almost perfectly encapsulated our mood.

'We could do something like that,' said Jules.

I loved that boy. He was never still. He thought three times as quickly as anyone else, talked three times faster, laughed and raged three times as often, burning up so much nervous energy that he always looked half-starved, like some beautiful, penniless Romantic poet. He was constantly thinking of new ways in which he and I could step out of the dreary consensual world and into the forbidden brightness beyond. It was him who decided one night we should walk right round the stone cornice of the main school building, four storeys up in the dark. It was him who got hold of those two tabs of LSD, the first of many, which we took one October day on top of a hill and watched the whole red pile of Shotsford

House below us reveal itself to be nothing larger or more significant than a gaudy cake, iced in vulgar pink and white, and crawling inside with maggots. And it was him now who was proposing we become terrorists.

He suggested it on a Sunday afternoon, when we'd driven down to the coast in a beaten up old car the two of us had managed to acquire for a few quid from an elderly local. We'd stopped at a pub and were sitting outside in the sun. Gulls were wheeling above us. The forbidden beer was pure ambrosia, our forbidden white Cortina a celestial chariot that would carry us between the stars.

'We should do something like that,' Jules said. 'Get some guns and shoot the place up. Think of the impact! The whole rotten system would shake in its fucking boots.'

Shotsford House had a rifle range, and we knew that guns were stored in a metal cupboard in the basement corridor. Things were much more casual in those days. Nowadays an expensive boarding school like Shotsford has a whole team of uniformed security guards equipped with vehicles and radios, and each pupil has an individual room, complete with en suite shower. But we washed in communal bathrooms and slept on sagging mattresses in chilly dormitories, while the entire security of the great dark building around us was entrusted to a single elderly man from a local village who wandered round the place with a torch. His name was Eliot, and, for strategic reasons, Jules and I had made a friend of him.

So now, sitting there in the pub with seagulls wheeling above us, and our chariot waiting for our return, we made a plan. In the early hours of the last day of term, Jules would meet Eliot near the science block, some distance from the main building, and engage him in conversation long enough for me to saw through the padlock and get out the guns. Eliot was very fond of talking and didn't see school discipline as being part of his job. On the basis of previous experience, we could be quite confident that, at the end of their conversation, he'd just tell Jules to go to bed and carry on with his rounds. Jules would then meet me in a hiding place of ours under the roof: a disused storeroom with a tiny window which we normally used for smoking out of, but from which it was possible, with a bit of effort, to squeeze out onto that high stone cornice. In the morning, when the parents came purring up the drive in their Jaguars and Rovers to pick up their darling boys, we'd be up there to greet them. Our backs against the sky, we'd fire down on them like avenging angels.

'Are we just talking here, Jules, or are we serious?' I asked, coming back from the bar with two more pints, and a new packet of rolling tobacco.

Jules was beautiful in my eyes, and I in his and we ached with desire for one another. We never expressed that desire in words, let alone through actual sex, and maybe I'm just repressed but I don't think I would even have wanted that. But every touch was a delight, and when we were together, it was as if we lit up the whole world.

Jules grabbed the tobacco and ripped off the cellophane, and we each tugged out a moist bundle of treacly strands. That stuff was especially delicious when it was completely new.

'Let's do it,' he said, as he exhaled his first rich cloud of smoke. 'Come on, let's really do it. I mean, why not? Apart from fear, what reason is there to hold back?'

Various answers do now suggest themselves to me – the desire not to kill people who had done us no harm, just to pluck a for-instance from the air – but at the time his question was rhetorical, and the moral objections carried so little weight that we didn't even speak of them. The following week I stole a hacksaw from the metalwork room and experimented with it on various pieces of iron-mongery to see how much time I'd need and how much noise I'd make.

But then Jules got talking to someone in the gun club and discovered that it was actually only air rifles that were stored in that metal cupboard, and that there was no ammunition there at all. Everything suddenly became rather dreary and complicated, and the whole project simply petered out.

I guess we wouldn't really have done it anyway. Neither of us were psychopaths. On the contrary, we were both in our own way the kind of people who have a strong need to do *good*. When I was expelled a year later, I went to work in a school in Africa and, from that starting point, gradually built up a career in international development. Jules, always more radical and daring than me, rebelled against rebellion itself, finding God, and celibacy, and submission to authority. He trained for the Catholic priesthood, fighting heroically all the time against doubts and forbidden longings. He was working in a dismal council estate in Liverpool when his ferocious inner struggle finally became too much for him, and he killed himself at the age of 28.

'I don't know what I believe in any more, Matt,' he said to me in a letter shortly before he died. 'I know I don't believe in God or the church. I *think* I believe in trying to make things better. But if you don't know what this world is or how it works, how *can* you make things better? How can you be sure you're not making things worse? It's like there's this huge machine towering over us, sucking people in, mangling them and spitting them out, and I know I'm part of it, I know I'm tainted by what it's doing, and I badly want to make it stop, but I've no idea which are the levers that turn it off and which make it go faster still. And the hardest part is that even my own motives are unclear to me, my own levers. I don't trust my impulses. I don't trust my judgement. Whatever I decide to do, I find myself wondering: who am I really doing this *for*?'

I know what he meant. Flying between international development conferences around the
world, or hurrying from one meeting to the next
along third-world roads in air-conditioned SUVs, I
too often ask myself who it is I'm really helping. I too
worry that my work may be perpetuating the very
problems that it is supposedly there to solve.

We were seeking purity back then at Shotsford. We
saw and loathed the blatant hypocrisy of our own
class, its smug self-righteousness, the way it wallowed
snout-deep in the trough of privilege even while
it flattered itself it was the humble servant of the
greater good, and we wanted to root that out from
inside ourselves. You couldn't have it both ways, that
was our view, and I think deep down it's my view
still. (Sometimes, I swear, sitting at some middle
class dinner table and listening to the conversation
move from tongue-clucking at the xenophobia of
ordinary English voters, to talk about how to get our
kids into the schools where the middle class kids do
well, my trigger finger still itches.) You couldn't call
yourself the enemy of capitalism if you remained
one of its beneficiaries, that's what Jules and I felt.
You couldn't be rich and enter the Kingdom of
Heaven.

My parents and Jules' were very comfortably off.
They had big cars that purred, and big houses that
women from small houses were paid to come in and
clean. Self-centred teenagers though we were, we

understood our complicity in all of that. We voluntarily attended the school they'd paid for. We bought our drugs and beer with the pocket money they provided. We lay dozing in our beds during the school holidays, while our parents' cleaners hoovered the rooms around us. We knew the enemy was inside us as much as outside, and it seemed to us that only self-destructive violence was a powerful enough emetic to purge it. What better way was there of finally separating yourself from a thing than making it hate you, having it hunt you down and fling you into its prisons? We hadn't heard of suicide bombing back then but, if we had, the thoroughness of the method would surely have appealed to us.

Purity was the thing. To destroy and to be pure. Anger is often a selfish emotion, the snarling of a dog that doesn't want to share its bone, but our anger seemed to us to be selfless, for we would throw away everything to serve it: our futures, our place in society, the pride of our parents, material wealth, the respect of our fellow citizens.

It was mostly narcissism, of course. It was mostly our own oedipal anger, inflated to the size of the world by our adolescent egotism. I've seen the same thing in my daughter Jasmine, screaming into the faces of policemen on anti-capitalist marches, and then coming home to upgrade her smartphone and book herself one of those intercontinental holidays that she and her friends dignify as *travelling*.

·

A few years after the London bombings, I was driving a hired Range Rover across the Republic of Malawi in southern Africa. I'd been visiting a series of projects across the region and was now returning to Lilongwe, the capital, where I had a number of meetings scheduled with senior figures in various NGOs. After several weeks of lodging in sticky rooms with no air conditioning and only intermittent electric power, I was very much looking forward to a few nights in a hotel with regulated temperatures and proper beds before finishing my business in the country and returning to the UK.

The landscape I'd been driving through was flat, and not particular scenic. It was largely denuded of indigenous vegetation, and dotted untidily with sparse dry plots of maize and vegetables, and little clusters of huts, reminding me of a scalp from which the hair has not so much been cut or trimmed as pulled out in clumps. There were people everywhere. From the horizon behind me to the horizon ahead, a steady stream of pedestrians was trudging stoically along the edges of the road, often with bags of charcoal on their heads, or bundles of branches. Evidence of any kind of indigenous economic development was minimal. In the larger settlements I passed through, the most prominent buildings typically housed projects funded by international NGOs – Oxfam, Christian Aid, *Médecins sans Frontières* – whose logos succeeded one another on the signs by the roadside.

I was finding all this rather depressing. No doubt these projects were appreciated by the people that used them, and no doubt they provided a pretty good living to many people, including me, but the message they gave out was very clear: the people of this country cannot look after themselves. Back in the donor countries the message was the same: pathos-drenched fundraising ads depicted sweet but helpless Africans, waiting for rescue with big brown beseeching eyes. How many local initiatives had been stifled, I wondered, how much inward investment had been lost, by the steady drip-drip-drip of this message over the decades?

I pulled over at a petrol station by a crossroads, asked for my tank to be filled up and bought myself a Coke.

'*Mazungu! Mazungu!*' children called out excitedly, as I climbed out of my car.

I sighed. This is a generic name for white people that's used across Malawi, Tanzania, Kenya and the whole Great Lakes area. I'm told the word originally meant something like 'aimless wanderer' and, at that particular moment, this actually felt about right. I *was* an aimless wanderer. I knew the road to Lilongwe, and the address of my hotel. I knew the time of my flight back to Heathrow. I knew where to send my expenses form when I got home. But I'd lost all sense of the purpose of my life.

There was a white plastic table outside the petrol station, with white chairs around it of the kind that people sometimes have in their gardens back in England. I took my Coke over there so I could sit down to drink it, and I also took a book I was reading, though I knew this wasn't the kind of place that a *mazungu* could expect to be left in peace. The children gathered in a group, about ten yards away from me. There were five of them aged about six or seven, two of whom were carrying baby siblings on their hips, and of course they were all very smiley and sweet. Now they watched me intently, beaming with anticipation, as if they thought I might at any moment grow wings and fly, or take water and turn it into wine. I waved and smiled to them, which made them squeal and laugh, running away for a few yards in pretence of being alarmed, and then creeping back again.

Presently a beggar approached me. He had wild red eyes, wore rags like some kind of mad John the Baptist, and was tightly clutching two live swallows. They dangled from his fist by their wings in a trance of terror and pain, while he waved them angrily in front of my face. Deciding that the birds were hostages rather than objects for sale, I gave him a few pence to take them away somewhere and let them go, and pretended to myself that I didn't know their wings would be too badly crushed for them to be able to fly.

'*Mazungu! Mazungu!*' the children called out again, completely untroubled either by the beggar in his rags or the suffering of his tiny captives.

I waved at them again, and once more they laughed and squealed and ran. We seemed to be playing a sort of reverse version of Grandmother's Footsteps, in which they ran when I looked at them, and stood still when I didn't.

Two young men came up to me, both wearing beautifully pressed white shirts and immaculate black trousers, and asked if I minded them joining me. Inwardly I sighed, for over the years I had been approached by many immaculately shirted young men in places like this. After a period of polite conversation, I knew, they would ask for my email address. And then, sometime later, I'd receive courteous requests from them for money, often couched in pious terms: 'I pray to Almighty God that you will be able to assist me in my hour of need.' But I couldn't very well stop them sitting on the seats, so I told them they were welcome, and then opened my book in the hope of discouraging conversation.

'Excuse me, sir, might I ask if you are from England?' asked one of the young men, after a few seconds.

I glanced up at him. He was the chunkier one of the two, with big awkward limbs, and cheeks piebald with vitiligo.

'That's right,' I said, and returned to my book.

The little children watched in fascinated silence.

'God willing, I hope one day to study in England,' the young man said wistfully.

I gave way to the inevitable and abandoned my

attempt at reading. These young patronage-seekers were never anything other than polite, after all, and you could hardly blame them for trying to find a way out of a country with so little in the way of opportunities. I laid down my book, offered them both my hand, and asked them their names. The chunky one was called Godfrey. His more taciturn and more handsome friend was Joyous.

'We both of us want to study in England,' Godfrey went on. 'Of course it's very difficult for us, for until we've studied, how can we make money? It's very difficult indeed.' He sighed. 'So we just hope that Almighty God will send help, and perhaps a friend in England, who might—'

'May I ask what your book is about?' asked Joyous. He seemed irritated by his companion's fawning.

I handed him the book. It was a popular introduction to the science of climate change, a subject which I'd decided I ought to know more about. Joyous studied the cover for a moment – there was a photo of a crop of wheat that had been killed off by drought – flipped it over to read the back, then opened it at random to sample the contents. He had long lean fingers and I could see that he was an entirely different proposition from his companion: sharp, focused, full of energy, and not in the least deferential.

'Climate change,' he said. He had the most beautiful glossy panther-like skin. 'Yes, I've heard of this. The world is getting warmer.'

'That's it.'

'What does the book say about what will happen in this part of Africa?'

I hesitated. Malawi is one of the poorest and most densely populated countries in the world, without the mineral wealth of many African countries, and with precious little in the way of industry. Many villages have no electricity: you drive through them in the night and there are people sitting there in total darkness. Most of the country's population live by subsistence farming, and almost all of its meagre export income comes from agricultural products like tobacco and tea.

'The news isn't good, I'm afraid,' I said. 'Global warming would probably mean a lot less rain round here, and a lot less certainty about when the rains will come.'

'Then we'll starve,' Joyous stated flatly.

'Why does God keep punishing us so much?' Godfrey murmured. 'I only wish we knew.'

'Well, let's just hope it doesn't happen,' I said.

Joyous flicked through pages, pausing to study pictures and diagrams.

'And what does your book say is the cause of this problem?' he asked, though it sounded to me as if he already knew.

'Mainly the burning of oil and coal in the industrialised countries, over the last two centuries.'

I found a graph for him, showing the increase of CO_2 in the atmosphere since the industrial revolution in Europe, and the corresponding increase in average temperatures. Joyous laughed.

'So you people come here from America and Europe to instruct us how to improve our lives, but at the same time you are slowly killing us. Is that correct?'

'Well, certainly not deliberately, but—'

'When was it discovered that burning these things would cause this problem?'

Joyous was smiling in the way that some people do when they're very angry. Godfrey giggled nervously, trying to catch my eye so he could defuse his friend's alarming hostility.

'Oh a long time ago. I think it was in—'

'So, excuse me, sir, I don't wish to be rude, but why do you say you don't do it on purpose, if you know quite well what it is you're doing?'

'I guess that's a—'

'And when we are starving, will your countries apologise, and welcome us in?'

Some chance, I thought! Of course they wouldn't. Joyous surely knew that as well as I did. On the contrary, the harder things became around the world, the more the relatively well-off would protect their own, the more they would roll out the razor wire, the more they would turn their victims into enemies against whom they must defend themselves.

I looked at my watch, then picked up my Coke bottle to return it to the cashier. People are particular about bottles in Malawi. Moulded glass is too valuable to waste.

'I think the best thing,' I said lamely as I stood up, 'would be if we tried to prevent the problem in the —'

'Excuse me,' Joyous interrupted, 'I can see you need to go, but could you please answer just one more question for me. If you're killing us on purpose, why shouldn't we come to your countries and kill you?'

Godfrey gave a shout of appalled laughter. The watching children's eyes darted anxiously between Joyous's face and mine. They were no longer smiling. They didn't understand English, but they could see the tension.

'Take no notice of my friend, sir,' said Godfrey, giving Joyous a hearty slap on the back. 'He's always playing jokes.'

But that Joyous wasn't joking could hardly have been more obvious. He was accusing me, just as I once sought to accuse the Shotsford House parents as they purred up the drive in their expensive cars. Joyous's rage was uncompromised, though, unlike my own adolescent anger. The thing he wanted to fight wasn't inside him, but truly out there in the world. He had no need to declare war on himself.

As I continued along the road, I wondered if this was a portent of things to come, for when a person has a new idea, they are hardly ever the only one. I felt ashamed, knowing that in the eyes of Joyous, I epitomised precisely the kind of hypocrisy that I myself used to despise. But, more than anything else,

I felt envy and grief. Envy for the purity of that young man's rage. Grief for the fire that Jules and I had sought, but never really found.

Roundabout

Two faces look out from a windscreen: Ralph's on the passenger side, Eve's above the wheel. They're not speaking to each other. In fact they haven't really spoken for this entire holiday. They've exchanged practical information when required, agreed on outings, sorted out meals, but there's been no communication between them about themselves.

There's a reason for this, which Ralph knows and Eve doesn't. All she knows is that Ralph is absent – not unpleasant, not unhelpful, but simply absent – and that this absence is of a new quality. Something or someone beyond her field of view, some powerful gravitational force, is tugging his attention constantly away from her. When she asks Ralph a question and he answers, it's as if a receptionist has been left in charge of his voice, quite polite most of the time and sometimes positively solicitous – as receptionists can be, when they sense that a caller is becoming annoyed – but never authentically Ralph.

'There's something on your mind,' she says now. 'Something you're not telling me.'

He laughs, but it's a laugh that's been deliberately chosen from a range of options, as if from a set of dials or sliders: Volume 3, Warmth 1, Nonchalance 10. 'As I keep saying, it's just the usual stuff. Work worries. What's going to be waiting for me when I go back on Monday. All of that.'

'There's something else.'

'I need a weewee,' says Lily's voice from the back.

In the parked car, Ralph takes out his phone.

'Ianthe, it's me! I had to call. How are you?' Even the simple word *you* is magical when he says it to her. 'It seems *so* long. So long since I saw you last, so long before I see you again. Two whole days! I'm counting off the hours.'

As he listens to Ianthe's reply, he peers out through the windscreen at the main entrance of a motorway service station.

'Yes, I know,' he says, his face a little crestfallen. 'I know I must. But I really can't do it now. Lily's with us all the time. I'll talk to Eve when we're back home. Listen, I'd better go. We only stopped so Eve could take Lily in for a pee. They'll be out in a minute. I can't wait to be with you, Ianthe. I... Oh, here they are now. Sorry, my dearest, but I've got to go.'

Ralph's face is impassive as he stares out at the road again, this time from the driver's seat. Calamity lies ahead, he knows, but he's oddly unmoved by it. All his usual loyalties are in abeyance, even his loyalty to his own future self. All his usual feelings are distant and muffled, as if behind soundproof padding. And if they do break through at all, he has simply to turn his mind to Ianthe – her smile when she sees him, the way she can't help herself from touching him, the words she says, her throaty laugh – and everything else is subsumed at once into a surge of sublime longing. *You*, he thinks, *you*, and the hills beside the motorway seem to smoulder in her golden glow. *Ianthe*, he thinks, *Ianthe*, and even this banal river of cars seems suffused with meaning.

He glances in his mirror, flips the indicator downwards, pulls out past a cargo of shipping containers.

But I need to decide what to do, he tells himself, as he presses down the accelerator.

He knows there's no way forward that doesn't involve pain. He understands that once he's told Eve what's been going on, the golden trance will end. Eve and Lily are remote from him now, far away behind that soundproof padding, but once they know the truth, they'll smash their way through, their own emotions far too powerful to be kept at bay. And even Ianthe will make new demands on him.

That's already starting to happen, actually. Up to now, his desires and Ianthe's have been so perfectly aligned, that to submit to hers has been to indulge his own. It's been possible to be magnificently generous and greedily selfish both at the same time, to receive boundless gratitude for gratifying himself. But now, as he replays that snatched phone conversation in

his mind, he can't avoid the impatient edge in Ianthe's voice. He called her for a heroin-like shot of
numbing love, but she reproached him for keeping her waiting. And the reproach still stings, even
though it's him she says she longs for.

But her circumstances are not identical to his.
She's had to think of him going to sleep beside Eve
and waking up beside Eve in the morning, while
Ralph's not had to imagine her with anyone but
friends and workmates (though actually he envies
even them). And there's no calamity ahead for Ianthe either, no one whose life she must devastate in
order to be with him. So Ralph has always had more
of an interest than her in prolonging this golden
limbo, this little eddy swirling round and round at
the margins of the stream of time. He has never
experienced such intensity before in this life, and he
knows he may never experience it again. There have
even been moments when he wondered whether
this thing itself is what he most craves, not Ianthe,
but this incredible intensity, this centrifuge of love.
Of course, he's always rejected this thought as soon
it came to him. And, in any case, Ianthe is growing
impatient. Whether he likes it or not, the golden
limbo is coming to an end.

So there will be ugly practicalities now, money to
be divided up, contact with Lily to be negotiated. He
will have to deal with competing claims on his time
and his loyalty, and face friends and relatives with
the news of his callousness and duplicity. And then

there will be this little family for him to grieve over, when he can no longer kiss his daughter goodnight every evening, or hear her cheerful voice calling out in the morning to announce the good news of her awakening.

Ralph can even see that, in this new world, his feelings about Ianthe herself will change, and hers about him. The two of them may be golden now in each other's eyes, but gold derives its value from scarcity, and their seemingly identical desires up to now have been the product of the tiny and simplified universe, that little glowing nest outside of time, in which they have conducted their secret relationship. That *is* the centrifuge, after all, that's how it works, whirling round and round to separate out pure golden desire from everyday ordinariness. He and Ianthe have both spoken of how they long to spend more time together, meet each other's friends, walk hand in hand in the streets without fear of being seen, but the truth is that everything will be different when the two of them emerge into the world under the sky. Her only just barely noticeable sharpness on the phone was a harbinger, the tip of a chisel that will prise apart two halves of a golden globe of mutual longing and turn them back into separate human beings, with their own histories, priorities, foibles. It's quite likely, Ralph thinks bleakly, that in the long run they will come to something not so different from the way things are with Eve.

It's not the first time he's thought this. Right from

the beginning of his affair with Ianthe, there's been a calm observer inside him, watching, noticing the dynamics, wondering at the melodrama of it all. The Czar dreams of new and golden lands. The peasant, to whom the fighting will actually fall, wonders what benefits, if any, will really flow from all that spilt blood and spent treasure. But the peasant has no influence in the polity of Ralph's mind, for he and Ianthe in their golden nest have told each other that they can be Czar and Czarina forever, and, as is often the case with Czars and Czarinas, no one has had the the power to contradict them.

But never mind all that, Ralph instructs himself. And, as he pulls out round another lorry, he pushes practicalities aside and begins to calculate once more the precise number of hours it will be before he is able to see her again, touch her skin, hear her voice, bask in the words she says to him: 'You're the love of my life, Ralph. You're all I think about. You're—'

'Lily's asleep,' says Eve, glancing back at their daughter in her car seat.

'That's good.'

'So you can answer my question, Ralph. What *is* it that you're not telling me?'

Again he laughs. Warmth 0, this time round, Nonchalance 12, and, for good measure, he nudges the slider for anger up to 3. It's a defensive anger in reality, the anger of a creature that's been spotted in its hiding place and is under threat, but Ralph so fervently needs it to be heard as the righteous anger of a falsely accused innocent, that he actually does *feel* righteously angry. Preposterous as the peasant knows this to be, the Czar really does feel that Eve is making unreasonable demands on him.

'Don't let's go over this now, Eve. It's not the moment. I'm tired and I'm driving at seventy mph on a motorway in heavy traffic. I need to concentrate on what I'm doing.'

He glances in her direction for half a second, sees her narrowed eyes watching him, and flinches. Is this going to be his future when he emerges back out under the sky? Eve, Ianthe, Lily: all three of them disappointed in him, all three of them asking him to deliver something he doesn't know how to give?

'We can talk when we get home,' he mutters. 'I promise. Is that alright? Will that do?'

'Now's not the time for *what*, that's what I want to know? What exactly *is* this thing that we're going to talk about then but can't talk about now? Why can't you at least tell me what it is?'

'I've got a lot of worries at work. You know that.'

He feels Eve's gaze searching his face, trying to catch a glimpse of him through the layers of armour plate.

'Well,' she says slowly, 'I don't know what's been happening at your work because you never tell me anything any more, but you've certainly been working late a great deal.'

'*Exactly!*' Ralph shouts, just barely managing to stretch his rage out far enough to cover up his panic.

For Eve is almost there. She's a single step away from naming what's going on. She only has to ask one more question, and the calamity will have begun. '*Exactly!*'

The truth is though, that Eve, too, is afraid of that next question. She too hesitates to rupture the thin membrane that still maintains the outward appearance of normality, and plunge the three of them into new and terrifying territory. So she asks a less specific question instead.

'Why are you so *angry* with me, Ralph?'

'For going on and on! When I've already said I need to concentrate on driving! Our daughter's in the back, in case you'd forgotten. Our precious daughter.'

This is a new low. He hears himself, appalled. Yet, bizarrely, he really does feel indignation, even though he knows it's entirely spurious.

'You've had every evening to talk to me the whole of this last week, after Lily went to bed,' Eve points out. 'But you just watched TV every night, and waited until I'd gone to sleep before you came to bed.'

'I just want to concentrate on driving till we get home,' he stubbornly repeats.

'I wonder what you'd do,' Eve says, 'if you knew *I* was holding something back from you, and I refused to say what it was? Would you be content just to let me drive? I don't think you would, you know. It seems to me that—'

'I feel sick,' whines Lily from the back.

'Poor darling,' says Eve, twisting round in her seat. 'I thought you were asleep!'

'She was,' says Ralph, in the aggrieved tone of one whose sensible warnings have all been ignored, 'but now you've woken her.'

'We're going to stop soon, sweetheart,' Eve tells their daughter.

'Remember we said we'd stop at the seaside for a bit, darling?' Ralph joins in, in a voice that strives to be even kinder and more solicitous than Eve's. 'It's not long now. It's not long now at all.'

The rusty skeleton of a seaside pier is cut off behind a razor wire fence. The beach consists of grey mud. Most of the buildings along the front are empty and boarded up, blank sheets of metal or plywood bolted on over the windows of what were once guesthouses and amusement arcades. They look like blinded eyes.

'This was a mistake,' says Ralph.

Neither he nor Eve know this part of the country, and they chose this particular seaside town simply because it was at about the right point to break their journey.

'Well we promised Lily, so we'll have to do our best to make it fun.'

'Of course.'

As he pulls up the car on the seafront, Ralph's now constantly simmering anger is roused once again by Eve's implication that he might in some way be less attuned to his daughter's needs than she is.

'Here we are, Lily my lovely girl!' he calls out. 'Here we are at the seaside!'

One good thing about the unattractiveness of this dismal town: there are plenty of parking spaces.

They emerge from the car. They look around. It struggles on, this dying place, like some maimed animal run over by a truck, but still trying to drag itself to safety. In between those blank squares of metal and plywood there is still a chip shop of sorts, a Pound Shop, a place selling plastic buckets and seaside rock, and a single small amusement arcade. The arcade is called Yogi's Cave and it has a life-sized bear outside it, moulded in fibreglass. 'Welcome, folks!' says the bear, its smile fixed, the arcade machines bleeping and gurgling behind it. 'Come and play in my cave! It's bear-*i*-fic!' For the rest of their time here, its mechanical voice will be there in the distance, coming in every couple of minutes with one of three standard phrases.

'I guess no one needs seaside towns any more in the north,' says Ralph, 'now there are cheap flights to Ibiza and Corfu.'

Eve ignores this completely. If he's going to refuse to tell her what's on his mind, she isn't going to offer him the comfort of ordinary conversation.

'There's a roundabout over there,' she says shortly. 'Lily will like that.'

'Come on in, people, come on in!' calls out the bear behind them. 'Let's all have some fun!'

•

Assisted from the car by her mother, four-year-old Lily climbs down onto the promenade and assays the attractions of this new place with her sharp grey eyes. The markers of poverty and decay mean nothing to her, and, unlike her parents, she has no sense of having strayed into the territory of an aggrieved and hostile tribe. Her mental template of a seaside town is more circumscribed than theirs, and requires only a short list of specific facilities, all of which seem to her to be satisfactorily present. The drifts of litter don't trouble her, nor does the coiled dog turd over there by the metal balustrade. They don't please her, of course, but they have no wider significance. She simply looks away from them, and gives her attention instead to the fibreglass bear that talks, the cartoonish tinkling and bleeping from the little amusement arcade, and the roundabout which her mother has already pointed out as a destination. Her parents might look at all this and see a dying thing, a mockery, a cruel parody of fun, but Lily takes it all at face value. Her mother and father are here after all, and she trusts them to keep her safe.

'He-e-ey kids! Yogi here! Check out all the games in my cave!'

'Hello, silly bear!' shouts Lily, and laughs.

The roundabout is one of those miniature ones for small children, the kind with one tractor, one car, one double-decker bus, each with its own little steering wheel so the children can pretend they're driving. All the vehicles have friendly faces. There is a cheeky space rocket, for instance, and a brave fire engine with a determined frown. There are also a few animals among them: a big chicken, a pale blue elephant, a pretty pink horse with a golden harness and big blue long-lashed eyes.

'I want to go on the horse,' Lily says.

Ralph goes to pay the man in charge, who has black greasy hair and a thin pockmarked face, and is wearing one of those dark camouflage jackets you see on men who like to fantasise about war. He takes Ralph's money without a flicker of acknowledgement. Not that Lily cares. With Eve's help, she's already climbing up onto the horse. 'It's bear-*i*-fic!' says the fibreglass bear in the distance. A cold wind blows diesel fumes towards them from the roundabout's generator

'Hold on tight, darling!' Eve calls out to her. 'Take care!'

There are no other riders, no other children anywhere near, as the roundabout begins to turn, its lights rippling and its speakers tooting out a Mary Poppins medley. 'Spoonful of Sugar' segues into 'Chim-Chim Cher-ee' as Ralph and Eve stand in the drizzle on opposite sides of the ride, watching their daughter going round and round. They never even glance at one another.

Lily waves proudly to her mum and dad. She bounces up and down. She cranes round to look

at the riderless animals and empty vehicles, all cir-
cling round for no one's benefit but hers. Then she
throws back her head and laughs.

Lily's laughter on that little horse, her peals of
happy laughter: ten, twenty, thirty years later, they
will still echo in Ralph's mind when he lies awake
at night. He knows this already, even now, when the
original laughter is still there in front of him and
the roundabout is still turning to the merry tune
of 'Supercalifragilisticexpialidocious'. Numb as
he is, cut off as he is from his own feelings about
everything except the golden dream of Ianthe, he
knows that when the dream has passed, and the Czar
has been toppled from his throne, that laugh will
haunt him all his life.

When the roundabout stops, Ralph goes back to the
man in the military jacket.

'Another go, please, mate. In fact can you make it
a double turn this time?'

He glances briefly at Eve, but her attention is
fixed firmly and entirely on Lily, who has decided to
transfer to the little car for her next ride. Lily beams
at her father as she settles into the car and waits for
it to move. It's true that something in his face makes
her smile falter for a moment – something that was
still lingering there as he turned to her from her
mother – but when the roundabout starts up again,
she forgets all that and gives her full attention to the

car. And soon she's laughing again, her small hands busily turning the steering wheel this way and that, though it's connected to nothing at all.

Ooze

Go out into the middle of the ocean, turn vertically downwards, continue in that direction for two miles until you reach a place where there's no light and the bare muddy sediment stretches away in every direction like a desert. That's where you'll find Ooze. Not that Ooze herself knows where she is, or that there could be anywhere else. Not that she knows she's Ooze.

Ooze has no eyes or limbs, only a narrow body with a mouth at one end of it, an anus at the other and a spinal cord along its length. She is essentially a tube. Her brain is no more than a smallish swelling at one end of that spinal cord. She can't think as we can. She can't reflect or reason. But that doesn't mean she can't feel. She knows pain, she knows fear, she knows pleasure, and she experiences them all with no less intensity than we do. Or perhaps even with more, for Ooze has nothing to mediate her feelings. She can't say to herself 'This is just a feeling' or 'I feel this way now but it will soon pass.' Feelings are all she has.

Ooze may have no eyes but she has senses. She tastes the water around her. She knows which way her body is oriented in relation to the sea bed, though she doesn't know the thing below her *is* the sea bed, and doesn't even conceive of herself as inhabiting a world separate from herself. She's sensitive to even tiny fluctuations in the pressure of the water against her body, including the vibrations that we call sound. She can feel the touch of objects against her skin, and particularly against the nerve-rich ring that surrounds her jawless mouth. And she has another sense too, an electric sense – let's call it tingle – which alerts her to the presence of other living creatures, including other individuals of her own kind.

She does not conceive of them as individuals, though, or as her own kind. To her they are tingly presences that make her furiously angry, either by intruding on her own patch of mud, or by being in her way when she chooses to move.

Ooze doesn't conceive of herself as an individual either. To herself she is the entire universe, and, though I have spoken of her as 'moving', she doesn't really experience herself to be moving as we'd understand it. For how can a universe move? Where could it move to? Ooze just knows that by wriggling her body in a certain way, she can pull new water and mud into existence in front of her and push old water and mud into nothingness behind her.

Ooze is always hungry, and she is always anxious. The two are closely related. She is the universe, and therefore immortal, so her fears are not centred on the possibility of ceasing to exist, but the function they serve is precisely that of keeping her alive. She fears all the time that she will find nothing to eat, however much mud and water she calls into being. And even when she finds food, her constant worry is that those tingly things that fight will appear out of nothing, as they sometimes do, and take it away from her.

There really is very little to eat in Ooze's world. Nothing grows down there. Every source of nutrition comes from above and, unlike mud and water, it can't be summoned towards her by wriggling movements of her body. It simply appears. As a matter of fact, though Ooze doesn't know this, her food consists of corpses, sometimes whole, but more often in tiny fragments. Dead fish, dead seabirds, dead crustaceans, dead seals: they reach her after descending slowly through those two vertical miles of water. Often they have descended part-way and then become bloated up with gas and risen back towards the surface, only to descend once more when their guts burst open, or are breached by carrion eaters. All of them have passed through many different realms in their journey from the upper waters to the bottom of the abyss, and all have been gnawed, chewed and plucked at by the many creatures who wait for dead flesh at each different level from the sunlit surface to the sunless depths, just as Ooze herself waits down there at the bottom of everything. Each layer has its own particular specialists in the processing of dead meat.

By the time they come to rest in Ooze's realm, the animal corpses have usually been torn to pieces. In most cases they reach her as tiny specks and motes: single fibres, individual bones, solitary scales and teeth, which may have been churning around in the eddies and currents of the middle levels for days or weeks or months. They're too small to truly satisfy, but better than nothing at all, and nothing at all is pretty common too. Hungry and anxious, Ooze has often waited for weeks on end without the smallest scrap to eat. (Though of course she doesn't know of days or weeks, for the only rhythms she experiences are her beating heart and her pulsing gills.) All she can do is wait, tasting the water as it passes through her gills, feeling the flux and tremble of it against her skin.

Once a troop ship came down, holed by a torpedo. It was full of drowned corpses, freshly dead, and they had descended so quickly to the bottom that they hadn't been so much as nibbled by Ooze's competitors in the layers above.

Strange new currents rushed by for a little while, and for a long time after these had subsided, the groans and clicks of cooling metal intruded harshly into the near-silence of the abyss, while stirred-up mud that had lain inert for centuries gave the water a powerful tang for many miles around. There were new and unfamiliar tastes too, tastes of metal and ash and oil, that persisted even when the mud had settled and the clicks and groans had fallen silent.

Ooze's senses registered these things, but none of them triggered any of her store of innate or conditioned responses. So she remained in her characteristic resting state, lying completely motionless except for the steady opening and closing of her gills, in the middle of her current patch of mud. But as time passed, new and interesting flavours began to waft in her direction. She became alert, her muscles tensing as she warmed them up in readiness for activity, her head turning slightly from side to side to sample the delicious traces in the water around her. Soon she began to move, wriggling vigorously to pull the source of these flavours towards herself, and push into oblivion behind her the barren patch of mud which, up to now, she'd been guarding as jealously as a dragon on its pile of gold. The more she wriggled, the more excited she became. For beneath the tang of metal she was tasting flesh, flesh in an abundance she'd never previously known.

All around her, for a distance of several miles, many thousands of Ooze's own kind were also springing into alertness, abandoning current territories, and pulling that mysterious cornucopia of flesh towards themselves. Each one alone in its own universe, thousands of small tube-like creatures wriggled along converging radial paths across the mud, until their mouths came up against the hard surface of the sunken ship.

The taste was quite exquisite now, and of an intensity that none of them had experienced before. No physical obstacle was going to prevent Ooze, or any one of her kin, from trying to reach its source. Ooze slithered back and forth over the barnacled metal – or, as it seemed to her, she turned the entire ship this way and that – until she came to the breach in the hull that had split it almost in two. And there, with the slimy writhing bodies of countless others pushing in around her, she slid inside.

Thousands had died in that ship. They too were essentially tubes, creatures with a spinal cord, a mouth at one end and an anus at the other, and were in fact descendants of creatures very much like Ooze herself. But over the course of time their ancestors had acquired hands and feet and lungs, and much larger swellings at the front end of their spinal cords. But of course Ooze, who didn't even know she had a mother or a father, and had no notion of a universe beyond her own sensations, could not know that she was burrowing in the bodies of her own distant cousins. (In fairness to her, it's doubtful that if they'd lived and Ooze had been caught and laid before them, they'd have recognised their kinship with her any better than she did.)

Ooze had never encountered this much food. None of them had. There was more meat here than they could eat in a lifetime and yet there was still an urgency about consuming it, for now that they were tearing into it, the taste of the rotting flesh was spreading wider and wider over the abyssal mud, and many more of Ooze's kind, from ten miles away and more, were stirring into alertness, moving their heads from side to side as they located the source of the alluring new taste, warming up their muscles, and joining the great migration towards the wreck.

So much food. So much more than Ooze could eat, and yet soon it would all be gone.

Inside the ship, Ooze's relatives were already all over every corpse. They were inside too. They pushed and shoved as they gnawed away in there, yanking at chunks of meat that clung to the bone, shoving each other aside to reach the choicest and most aromatic morsels. In the pitch darkness, the dead soldiers and sailors jerked this way and that as if they were still alive. Their cheeks moved as if they too were chewing. Their bellies gave sudden jerks as if they were pregnant women with babies almost ready to be born.

Ooze couldn't think. She didn't make plans or devise strategies. But simple plans and strategies were pre-wired into her tiny brain, the legacy of success-ful choices made by her ancestors. (They were truly remarkable ancestors, by the way. Every one of them, without even a *single* exception, had been one of the tiny percentage of individuals in each generation who'd lived long enough to reproduce. If you met her she might not seem so, but Ooze was one of the crème de la crème.) And so, though Ooze herself was incapable of working out a solution to the problem of there being too much meat to consume before others came and took it from her, it was an old problem, and Ooze's body had a solution ready-made.

She began to feel a new desire. Where normally the touch and tingle of others round her would have made her irritable and anxious and prone to fight, now she longed to feel them closer still. She couldn't get enough of their slipperiness, the smoothness of their skin, the way their wriggling sent tremors, over and over, from one end of her little body to the other. She craved their touch, she ached for the electric tingle of their nerves. Soft, smooth, writhing flesh was already rubbing against her, making her quiver with ecstasy, but still she wanted more. And so she pressed against the others, coiled herself around them, slid her skin over theirs, until suddenly the pleasure became too much to bear and a jet of tiny eggs came bursting from her.

The same stimuli had been at work on all the others round her. They might be separate universes, islands of sensation in a void, but they were subject to the same basic laws, for each of them had ancestors every bit as distinguished as Ooze's own, each was a member of the same tiny elite of the living. And so, as she spurted out eggs, they spurted too, until the water inside the wreck was thick and soupy with tiny gritty eggs and chlorine-tasting nebulae of creamy milt.

There was no plan on Ooze's part, or on the part of any of the others, there was no strategy, but nevertheless an impeccable strategy was unfolding. Very soon millions of tiny fry were jiggling about in the clouded water, seeking out the dead flesh that they could already taste and recognise, though they as individuals had never encountered it before. They fastened themselves onto the ragged remnants of the soldiers and sailors, their tiny bodies forming great quivering sheets that pulsated in unison as they sucked and rasped at muscle and connecting tissue, skin and fat, guts and eyes and brains. Where bones had been broken by the explosion that had destroyed the ship, even the marrow was consumed, as the fry pressed through the jagged fractures and swarmed into the rich interior flesh, pulsing, quivering, jiggling, as they sucked and chewed and grew.

Ooze and her fellows might not be able to do justice to all that meat, but they could make copies of themselves who could.

And then quite suddenly the meat was gone. The ship was left with a crew of skeletons whose uniforms enclosed body-shaped masses of empty water, and whose bones tasted of nothing more appetising than chalk. The only taste in the water now was metal, and ash, and the drifting faeces of Ooze and all the others, the last remnants of the meat, which would spread out across the abyssal plain, settle onto the mud, and be processed in turn by the microscopic lifeforms out there that specialised in such things.

From being a place of plenty the ship had all at once become exceptionally barren, a place that would yield no food at all, without even the usual meagre possibility of scraps descending from the surface. Ooze knew this, though the knowledge wasn't encoded in her limited store of learned information, but in the wants and impulses that had been built into her brain over all those millions of generations of successful ancestors.

She didn't want to be here any more: that was the form her knowledge took. She didn't know why – she didn't even know of the possibility of asking why – but she knew she didn't want these tastes around her, and that she disliked the troubling vibrations that resulted from being enclosed. What was more, these tingling, wriggling presences all around her no longer provoked desire. She had no recollection of their ever having done so, nor any understanding that many thousands of them were her own sons and daughters. All she knew was that the proximity of all this touch and tingling once again provoked the feelings that it normally would: worry, irritation, fury, dread. And those feelings were a kind of knowledge too, not the temporary surface knowledge that is acquired in a single life, but a deep and ancient knowledge that was as much part of her make-up as her mouth or her senses or her spinal cord. Ooze could not reason, but the laws of her body, based on the experience of countless generations, were reasonable. One could say that Ooze's body knew, even if she did not, that too many rivals in too small a space would very soon mean starvation.

She pushed the cold metal and the bone away from herself, pushed and turned, until taste and water flow and sound showed her which way she needed to face in order to find mud and open water which she could pull towards herself. And so, in due course, little wriggling Ooze emerged once again from the stripped and scoured wreck. All around her, thousands of tingling others were doing the same, wriggling over and under one another in their hurry to escape. Hunger would very soon build up. Even out there, in the open water around the wreck, there was nothing like enough nourishment descending from above to feed so many mouths. In this now hopelessly overcrowded part of the abyss, every tiny scrap of food that came down from the nothingness above would find a thousand hungry squirming rivals rushing to be the first to reach it.

And that meant that, out of every thousand, nine hundred and ninety-nine would soon be dead, their bodies fought over and torn apart by the still living, most of whom would die and be eaten in their turn. Nothing was wasted down there on the mud, nothing that could be eaten was left to lie.

But with her belly still full for the moment, Ooze pushed the useless metal and bone behind her with a firm rhythmic movement of her narrow body, and pulled the open mud steadily towards herself. Half a mile, a mile, she kept on moving, a tiny wriggling shape on a vast featureless expanse. It was chance, most probably, that sent her far enough away from the wreck to find a defendable territory that would be big enough to keep her going. It was probably just luck that she got away before being completely hemmed in by rivals who wouldn't let her cross their mud. But chance or not, she got out in time.

And now she waits there again at the bottom of the abyss for the scraps and fragments that appear from above. She is always hungry, always anxious, always on the edge of murderous rage, but yet she is still alive. If she were like us, she'd look back fondly on the times of plenty, that happy interlude when there was more meat than she could eat, those precious moments when her body was so full of pleasure that her own substance burst out from inside her into the surrounding water. But old Ooze isn't one for memories. Just as the point in space which she occupies is the centre of the universe, so each moment is the only moment she knows.

Yet she has learnt one thing from the time of the ship, learnt it in something like our own sense of that word, I mean: learnt it with her own brain in her own lifetime. She's learnt that the taste of metal and oil and ash means meat. It means meat in abundance, still unchewed. And it means pleasure, ecstatic pleasure, pleasure of every kind.

Ooze doesn't think about that taste again, because thinking isn't a thing she does. She doesn't play it over in her mind. She doesn't revisit it. But if she ever encounters it again, she won't wait this time for the taste of flesh to follow. No, if a lump of burnt metal descends again to her part of the abyss, clever Ooze will head towards it at once. She will drag it closer to herself, haul it out of nothingness, draw it into the tingling core of the universe, so that the universe may be transfigured once again by joy and exultation and rapturous pleasure.

To say Ooze *hopes* this will happen again would be to impose our kind of understanding on hers. And yet this new readiness, this new reflex, newly conditioned into her modest brain, is a kind of analogue or prototype of hope. She doesn't know it, she doesn't know it at all, but what Ooze hopes for in this prototypical and unconscious sense is that her strange-limbed cousins in the world above will sink more of their ships, or crash their planes, or have their great cities flooded by tidal waves of sufficient power to fling cars and buses and trains far out into the sea, so that little Ooze can gorge herself, down at the bottom of the world, and be happy once more before she dies.

Newmarket

This was their third date and Judy had suggested a walk not far from where she lived, followed by lunch in a local pub. It wasn't the ideal day for it, Gerry privately thought, and he wasn't so keen either on her choice of walk. Under a low grey sky, the country around them was flat not only in the sense of having no hills but also, so it seemed to him, in the sense of being 2D, as if not only colour but the third dimension had somehow been leached out of it. And, in this austere, minimalist landscape, Judy had chosen the most minimalist of landscape features to walk along. It was apparently once a defensive barrier, thrown up in the Dark Ages to protect the East Angles from enemies to the west, but that didn't alter the fact that it was a dead straight bank of earth beside a dead straight ditch.

'Think of the labour it must have entailed,' said Gerry, trying to work up an interest. 'No diggers, no bulldozers, no trucks. Just human beings with picks and spades and baskets.'

It was a very conventional observation to make in such a spot, no more exciting really than the landscape itself, and it had probably been made in this exact same place many thousands of times before. But Gerry's theory about conversations was that they were like jazz. You might start out with a simple chord sequence or a banal melody, but you built things up collaboratively from there. This had seemed to work quite satisfactorily on the last two dates, and, although Judy was a somewhat less confident soloist than he was – he was a science fiction writer, after all, and riffing on ideas was in a way his job – she had seemed to enjoy the game of starting with a simple theme and ending up in new and unexpected places.

Today, however, she remained silent.

'And all for what?' added Gerry. 'Nobody now remembers which side of this line their ancestors came from, or what the fight was about that necessitated all this work.'

'Well, I expect it was useful at the time,' Judy said.

It was a reasonable comment he thought. In fact, it was rather an interesting one if you stopped to think about it. Barriers *were* useful. Indeed, they were absolutely fundamental, because…

But there was something about her tone that made him feel reproached. 'Let's not go off on yet another of your rambles, Gerry,' it seemed to say. So he didn't pursue the subject any more, though he wondered a little resentfully what exactly *was* interesting about this bloody ditch, if one wasn't allowed to think about its history or its purpose.

Their talk moved on to more everyday matters –
work, their respective kids, her family in Bristol, his
ex, places they'd been and people they knew – but
he felt that reproach still, lurking there behind
everything else she said. She'd seemed to enjoy his
company on their last two meetings, but this time,
there was no doubt about it, Gerry was getting on
her nerves. In fact, having developed a feel for the
life cycle of these encounters, he thought it quite
likely that this would be the final date. It was as if
he was a new shoe, which Judy had found quite
comfortable when she first put it on, but now was
starting to pinch and chafe. Most probably she'd ask
the assistant to take it back and fetch her another
pair. He felt sad about that.

After a couple of miles, the dyke was bisected by
a busy dual carriageway, which they crossed via a
footbridge. Engines snarling, tyres hissing, cars and
trucks hurtled beneath them at 70, 80, 90 miles an
hour, half of them rushing eastwards, the other half
heading west with equal urgency. This struck Gerry
as mildly amusing.

'All this self-important haste, in two opposite
directions!'

When Judy smiled faintly but didn't answer, he
felt a moment of mild panic. 'I'm sorry if I'm boring
you,' he almost burst out, 'but I'm just trying to have
a conversation.'

That would have been silly of course. It wasn't
as if they'd been walking in silence all this time.

They'd been having a perfectly reasonable chat about their kids and holidays and so forth, and Judy really wasn't obliged to respond to every one of his observations about their surroundings, particularly the rather dull ones which were all he'd managed so far. What really *was* his point, for instance, about the dual carriageway? That roads should only go one way? That no one should go anywhere at all? That everyone should travel round together in a herd? (It was typical of Gerry that he enumerated these alternatives in his mind, and briefly weighed each one.)

On the far side of the bridge, there was a stile in a hedge, and beyond that, suddenly and, to Gerry, completely unexpectedly, there was a large and very famous race course, with hundreds of acres of mown grass, and miles and miles of white railing.

A bit of the dyke had been levelled out to let the race track through, and they had to cross over there to climb back onto the earthwork. Once they were up on top again, they could see a starting gate, only about fifty yards ahead of them to their left. It was a long metal structure with rubber tyres which had been towed into place by a tractor and, to Gerry's surprise, racehorses were trotting up to it right now, with jockeys in multicoloured liveries casually chatting to one another as they brought the animals round into the stalls. Gerry knew nothing whatever about horseracing, but it seemed to him oddly informal and off-hand that a race should begin in this way, over here by the dyke, with no one to watch the horses set off other than him and Judy who just happened to be passing. And the jockeys didn't seem at all like the intense gladiatorial competitors he'd seen in sports page photos. They reminded him more of those delivery drivers whose job was to deliver cars to showrooms. They simply brought horses over here, it seemed, batch by batch, rode them back again as quickly as they could, and then fetched another lot.

But then again, he thought, who's to say that gladiators themselves didn't chat as they waited to enter the arena?

'You alright, Septimus?'

'To be honest, Lucius, I really could have done without this today. My bloody tooth is killing me.'

'I keep telling you, mate, you need to get that pulled! It won't get better by itself.'

'I know, but have you ever watched it being done? It must hurt like shit.'

'Of course it hurts, you wus, but then it's over and done with, isn't it? And you can stop thinking about it.'

'Yeah, but knowing my luck, I'd get the old thumbs down in the next fight, and then it would all have been for nothing.'

He didn't mention this imaginary exchange to Judy. He would have done on their previous dates – he would have put on accents and everything to make her laugh – but his instinct was that it just wouldn't work today. It wouldn't be funny enough. It would come over as grey and 2D, like everything else.

A simple admission of ignorance, however, would surely be in order.

'This is going to sound stupid,' he said, 'given that I now live only about ten miles from here, but I'd always assumed that a race course would be lined with excited spectators all along its length.'

It just seemed all wrong to him that, apart from himself and Judy, who hadn't even come here for the race, and a couple of officials beside the gate, the horses and jockeys were completely on their own. The white rails of the track headed diagonally away from the dyke across a great empty expanse of mown grass. And yes, now that he looked he could see in the distance a big concrete grandstand full of people, but it was a mile away from here, a different place entirely, the people just dots, the stand itself like a toy.

But then the gates opened and the horses were off, running together in a group between those lonely white rails, and Gerry realised he'd been wrong to imagine that there was no one here to take an interest. Almost at once a strange sound started up in the distance from the far side of that empty expanse of grass. It was brutal and primitive, an ape-like hooting, harsh and violent, that rose in intensity to a kind of peak, and then stopped completely all at once, as the horses passed the distant stand, and crossed the finishing line.

In the silence afterwards, giant amplified voices boomed out, soothing the crowd and instructing it.

He couldn't hear the words – they were all scrambled up by being repeated by many different loudspeakers that were out of sync with one another – but their authority was unmistakable.

Gerry turned to Judy with a smile.

'Who needs science fiction, eh? Who needs imaginary planets? What could be more alien than planet Earth?'

She glanced at him, but then looked back at the distant stand. He was *really* getting on her nerves that afternoon.

'Oh come on, Gerry. It's just people. Just a bunch of ordinary people, having a bit of fun with their friends. What's so wrong with that?'

'Nothing's wrong with it, Judy. Nothing at all. That wasn't my point at all. I was just noticing how strange it was.'

Good God, he had no objection to people having fun! People needed all the fun they could get in this grey, flat, empty world. And if they could cheer and yell and get excited even in this dreary place, about something so fundamentally dull and trivial as a bunch of running animals with men on their backs, well, all credit to them.

He turned to face her.

'You're finding me irritating today, aren't you, Judy?'

There were more announcements from the loudspeakers in the distance. These voices that they could hear from a whole mile away were truly giant-like in their reach, and yet they seemed small and inconsequential in this great hollow space under the sky, just as the race track itself did.

'Not really, but I just don't see why you have to *mock* everything all the time.'

More horses and riders were already trotting out towards them across the grass.

'Mock? I certainly don't mean to mock.'

'Well, okay, maybe *mock* isn't quite the right word. But you always seem to want to drill down through everything that people do, examine it, take it to pieces, and you never seem satisfied until you've got to the point where whatever thing it is you're talking about just looks silly and meaningless. It's... I don't know... It's as if someone were to show you a book, and you couldn't help yourself from pointing out that it was really just wood pulp and ink, or that words were really just arbitrary sounds. Why not just read the words and enjoy what they have to say?'

Gerry laughed. 'That's a fair point, actually.'

Why *was* he always so unwilling to take things at their face value? Why *did* he always feel the need to step back from whatever was going on and see it from a different angle to everyone else? Judy had seen him as mocking, but the truth was that he admired and envied the ability of others to engage with the everyday world on its own terms, and he often berated himself for not being more like them. Judy herself was a paediatrician – she was Dr Judy Fotherington at work – and when she talked about what she did, he was amazed by the scale of the problems she had to resolve every working day, weighing up possibilities, dealing with distraught people, and, hour after hour, choosing courses of action that might change whole lives for better or for worse. He knew her job would terrify him. He knew that, unable to face the responsibility, his mind would keep skittering away. And then something would go wrong, and it would be his fault.

They talked about other things now, a sister of Judy's who'd not been well, Gerry's son who'd been having problems at school, and it wasn't until later, when they turned to walk back again, that he returned to her point.

'I really don't *experience* myself as drilling down in search of meaninglessness, Judy. Quite the opposite, in fact. I feel myself to be seeking meaning.'

When they were back alongside the starting gate again, with its rubber tyres, they stopped to watch another race begin. Gerry recognised some of the riders and liveries from before. That red-headed guy, for instance, in the purple and green diamonds. It was the same riders, over and over, on a different set of horses.

There was meaning in the everyday world, but it was made of gossamer, that was how Gerry saw it. It could hold you up if you were very very gentle with it, but otherwise you fell right through. People like Judy accepted that fact, and treated the gossamer with respect. People like him had to keep tugging it and wriggling about, in search of something firmer, something they could get a grip on, something which wouldn't tear if they were clumsy, or restless, or felt like being a little rough. This wasn't necessarily the best strategy, he acknowledged. In all probability, there was nothing firmer to be found, and you either worked with the gossamer stuff and its limitations, or you were left with nothing at all. You went along with the game – *entered into it*, as people said, treated it like it mattered – or you stood on the side lines while others played. He was just a bystander. Others dealt with the world as they found it, got on with what could be done, and didn't waste their time on things that were beyond their power to change.

Judy was in front when they came to the bridge over the dual carriageway, and she walked straight across to the other side, but Gerry stopped in the middle to watch all those tons of metal rushing by beneath him, punching their way through the air as they hurried east or west. He had felt rebuked by Judy for wanting to dismantle everything. Recognising there was more than a little justice in what she said, he had felt cornered, and had promptly responded by dismantling *himself*. But now he was collecting himself again. He was giving himself some time. He was gathering himself together.

Gerry was good at getting out of corners. All this drilling down that Judy complained about, all this prodding and tugging at the gossamer, was Gerry's way of making sure that there would always be a way out, for it meant that wherever he happened to be was provisional, and there was the possibility of being somewhere else. If he couldn't escape the wolf on the ground, well then, he'd just become a swallow in the sky. If an eagle then dived towards him, he'd stop being a bird and become a fish instead. And if a shark opened up its jaws and rushed towards him, he'd banish the whole ocean and run off as a gazelle, leaping away across the plain, while the shark snapped its teeth in the surf.

Judy had stopped to wait for him on the far side.

'You okay?' she asked, as he joined her.

'Yes, of course, I'm fine.'

'You looked a bit troubled there, I thought, standing looking down at the cars.'

Gerry laughed. 'Sorry, Judy. The truth is you got me thinking, and it gave me an idea for a story. I was just quickly getting hold of it before it slipped away.'

'What? A whole story came to you? Just standing there on the bridge?'

With Gerry now walking in front, they climbed back up onto the dyke.

'Oh no,' he said, 'not a whole story at all, but, you know, a setting. A setting and a source of tension. Which is a good start. I was imagining that road as it might be one day, far off in the future, when you and me and the world we live in are as thoroughly forgotten as the people who built this dyke.'

'I guess people would still know it was a road, wouldn't they?'

'They would. And still use it as a road as well, as we still use Roman roads now that are hundreds of years older than this dyke. But the thing that really puzzles those future people about these kinds of road is that they actually consist of *two* roads running side by side. There's been some kind of catastrophe in England, you see – nuclear war, runaway global warming: I'll think of something or other – and there are no cars any more and not nearly so many people. So they look at that road back there and see that each carriageway is more than wide enough to take three big carts side by side, and they just can't imagine a volume of traffic that would justify two such big roads running together along the exact same route.'

The sky had become a little brighter, he noticed, and some depth and colour had returned to the landscape around them.

'So they actually only *use* one carriageway,' Gerry went on, 'that's what I was thinking. They only use the northern one of the two: the eastbound one as we'd call it now, though they travel on it in both directions. Most of the metalled surface has long since gone, but when holes appear they get filled in with gravel and the road is still the best and the busiest for miles around.'

'What about the other carriageway?'

'Ah, well that's going to be the point of the story. The southern carriageway they leave alone. They've allowed a thick barrier of trees and shrubs to grow along the edge of it and down the central reservation, so as to isolate it from its surroundings, and they never walk or ride on it at all except when they have to cross over it to take a turning south. Even then, their practice is to pass over it quickly, with eyes cast firmly down, not looking to the left or the right, and children are sternly warned not to peek.'

'Presumably they have some reason for this?'

'They certainly do. What they've decided, you see, is that the northern carriageway was intended for human travel and the other was meant for spirits. They call the southern carriageway the spirit road.'

'And the spirits are what? The dead?'

'Not just the dead. They use the word "spirits" to refer to things that seem to exist in some way but don't fit in with their understanding of the world. The people on the human carriageway can't deny the existence of spirits altogether, however much they might like to, because the world is full of mysteries and contradictions, but they've very sensibly given those troublesome spirits their own road to travel on, so they can go about their own spirit business to their hearts' content, and leave the humans undisturbed.'

'But really this spirit road is just the westbound carriageway of the A14?'

He beamed at her. 'That's right. That's a nice touch, don't you think? I'm really quite taken with it.'

'Yes, I quite like it too. I can see it has possibilities.'

'Most people don't have anything to do with the spirit road, except maybe the odd furtive glance when they have to cross over it. And that makes sense. It only unsettles them, and what use is it to them, anyway? They've more than enough to do and to think about on the human road, where folk trade and chat and joke and argue, and make friends and all the rest of it. I'm sort of thinking *Canterbury Tales* in the thirty-fifth century when it comes to the human road: plenty to see, plenty to do, plenty of fun to be had, plenty of drama, plenty of problems to be solved.'

'But, let me guess, a few folk prefer the spirit road?'

'You're way ahead of me, Judy. It's strictly against all the rules to walk on the spirit road, but some people are drawn to precisely that emptiness and stillness that most are so keen to avoid. They wait for quiet moments on the human road, when no one will see them creep through the trees and shrubs, and then they go and look at it, or even step out onto it and feel the invisible traffic passing all round them. Imagine a whole carriageway with nothing moving on it, screened off from its surroundings by trees! Once in a while a bird alights on it, or a deer wanders across, or perhaps the trees on either side sway a little and sigh in the wind. But most of the time, it's completely silent. You can still hear all the sounds of the human road, of course, just on the far side of the trees – talk and chatter, shouts and yells, hooves and rumbling wheels – but, from the spirit road, all of that seems like another world.'

'What do those people call themselves? The ones who like the spirit side?'

'I'm not sure yet, but let's say Southroaders for the moment. To them, the stillness and emptiness of the spirit road is pregnant with possibilities. I guess that's what the spirits *are* really: possibilities, alternatives, things that are currently excluded from the human consensus on what's real and what's worth talking about. Sometimes, when the Southroaders creep out at night onto that empty carriageway, they even catch glimpses of a long-ago time, when there were so many red tail lights heading west that the road became a river of fire.'

Judy laughed. 'Okay, so now let me have another guess. The Southroaders – who, by the way, sound suspiciously like Gerry the sci-fi man – discover some amazing new thing which the Northroaders would never have come up with. And it helps everyone. And then the Northroaders are forced to admit they've been completely wrong to stick so rigidly to their side of the road.'

Gerry smiled and shook his head. 'No, Judy, the Northroaders *aren't* wrong. Not at all. They're the ones who get stuff done. And what's more, the Southroaders are only drawn to the empty road because there's something on the north side they don't quite get or can't quite face. All that activity and banter and hurly-burly, I suppose, all those

complicated and confusing games which require so
much commitment and concentration: it's all a bit
too much for them.'

'I think you're being a bit hard on them now,
Gerry. After all, you said yourself that most people were scared of the spirit road, and tried not to
even think about it. So, at least in some ways, it's
the *Northroaders* are the ones who are afraid to face
things, and the Southroaders who are brave and
bold.'

The walk was nearly over and the car park was in
sight.

'Well, I need to work on it,' Gerry said, as they
climbed down the steps at the end of the dyke.
'These things take time.'

Judy ran to catch up with Gerry as they walked the
last few yards to her car and, to Gerry's pleasure and
surprise, she slipped her arm through his.

'Maybe a couple of them get together,' she suggested. 'Someone who's at home on the north road
and someone who's happier with the spirits. Who
knows, they might even complete each other?'

Gerry smiled, and cupped his hand briefly over
hers before they got back into the car.

'It's a possibility, certainly. But it's all at a very early
stage and it still needs a lot more thought.'

The Great Sphere

Of course the city has long been famous as a place of
wonders. Even in medieval times, visitors enthused
about its fountains, colonnades and gilded spires.
But every visitor, then and since, seems to agree
that the greatest wonder of them all is the Sphere
of Truth. Some six metres in diameter and with its
entire surface packed tightly with images and hieroglyphs, it is recessed on a vertical axis into the face of
the cliff that forms the city's northern edge, so that
one side of the sphere is in full view, while the other
is hidden inside the rock.

I spent ten months over there in my youth, but I
never learnt to read the inscriptions myself. Many
years of study are required to master that uniquely
complex ideographic script, developed specifically
for the purpose of expressing abstract ideas in a
highly compressed form. (So that, for instance, a
single hieroglyph can represent 'The idea that, in
principle, human society is capable of improving
itself indefinitely', or 'The belief that human beings
should not necessarily be rescued from the negative consequences of their own actions', or 'The

proposition that subjectivity, rather than material existence, is at the core of the universe'.) However, the script was beautiful and the images even more so: diagrams, symbols, scenes from stories, all beautifully inlaid with enamel so bright that it almost seemed luminous. In more peaceful circumstances, I could have spent many hours quietly examining those pictures from the tiered galleries provided for that very purpose.

But during my time in the city there *was* no peace in the vicinity of the Sphere. It was a scene of constant conflict. So much so that, if set down in any part of the Cliff Quarter at any time of the day or night, I could easily have found my way blindfold to the Sphere, simply by listening out for the shouting and the angry screams. Even in the early hours of the morning (when, in those days, the Sphere was only illuminated by the weak flickering glow of nearby street lights) there were people in front of it hurling abuse at one another. During the day, larger numbers gathered, and I saw stones and rotten vegetables being flung, and sometimes full-scale fights between rival groups that might each be twenty or thirty strong.

What the people of the city were arguing about, and what their forebears had argued about for centuries, was the position of the Sphere on its axis. No one disputed that the artefact was precious, or that it was a repository of the city's wisdom, but what maddened people was that at any one time, half of that wisdom was beyond the reach of human eyes. Everyone knew that what was hidden was an alternative way of seeing the world that might challenge, or even overturn, the accepted wisdom that the Sphere now revealed.

One group favoured turning the Sphere in a clockwise direction from its present position, believing that this would expose certain much-needed truths that were now hidden in the rock. Once, quite soon after I arrived, I witnessed these Clockwisers myself as they very briefly gained the upper hand, set their shoulders against the Sphere's enormous bulk and managed to shift it slightly. The Anticlockwisers, though, soon put a stop to this. They wanted to turn the sphere too, but in the opposite direction, believing that it was on the left-hand side of the hidden hemisphere that the really important truths were hidden.

There was intense antagonism between these two groups, but each was also internally riven. Among the Clockwisers, a faction known as the Completers believed that only a short turn of a few degrees was required in order to fully expose truths that could currently only be glimpsed in partial form along the right-hand edge, but there were also Deepers, who believed the really important material was much further back and completely hidden. Similar divisions were present among the Anticlockwisers. What is more, within both the Clockwiser and Anticlockwiser camps, there existed revolutionary factions which believed that the position of the sphere should be *entirely* reversed: *everything* hidden should be revealed; *everything* revealed should be hidden. The Clockwise revolutionaries were called Reversalists, the Anticlockwise ones Renewalists, and they were said to hate each other with a great passion, in spite of sharing the same ultimate goal.

In addition to the various factions of Clockwisers and Anticlockwisers, though, there was a third whole group which believed that the side of the sphere currently revealed was the one that contained the really vital truths and the most beautiful images. Centuries of history, these people argued, had brought the Sphere, like the polity itself, to its perfect resting place, while the hidden side contained only flawed and outmoded ideas, which would only sow confusion if exposed to the light. This last group, known as the Achieved Perfectionists, was the largest of the three and, throughout the history of the city, had always been the dominant force. One reason for this was that the other two groups tended to cancel out each other's efforts, both being able to call on the Achieved Perfectionists as allies if their opponents looked like gaining the upper hand. The other reason was that the Achieved Perfectionists had always had the support of the city's elite, which, naturally enough, was suspicious of anything that might unsettle the established order.

There had been times indeed, and not so long before my stay there, when the Achieved

Perfectionists had used their political power to proscribe the activities of Clockwisers and Anticlockwisers, surrounding the Sphere with armed guards to prevent anyone from touching it (and so allowing visitors to examine it in peace, I couldn't help wistfully reflecting). This was no longer the case in my time – the law now protected the right of the various groups and factions to hold and express their views – but in practical terms the Achieved Perfectionists did still dominate. Over the ten months I spent in the city, I visited the artefact many times and, though I occasionally witnessed it being shifted a centimetre or two this way or that, a move in one direction was invariably followed by a move in the other. The image that was at the centre of the hemisphere when I first saw it was a group of male and female figures in brightly coloured robes, and it was in the exact same place, as far as I could tell, when I paid a final visit to the Sphere on the day I left the city.

Pictures of the Sphere were still strictly forbidden during my time there. Both making and possessing such images were very serious offences that attracted lengthy prison terms and it had only been comparatively recently – a matter of decades – that the penalty for both crimes had ceased to be death. Nevertheless, after leaving the city and returning home, I managed to find quite a number of pictures that had been made over the centuries in secret by more intrepid visitors than myself, and I discovered that, in spite of the dominance of the

Achieved Perfectionists, the Sphere did shift over time. A century and a half previously, for instance, a Swiss traveller named Anton Gustave Meuli had managed to disguise himself as a local trader and his bulky camera as a chestnut stall, and had risked the garrotte to take a blotchy daguerreotype which shows that group of robed figures in a position very definitely to the left of the central point. Three centuries earlier, the sixteenth-century Florentine painter Guiseppe Merccini produced an astonishingly detailed reproduction by memorising small sections of the Sphere's surface, one at a time, and running back and forth between it and his studio. He was eventually caught and duly executed – in fact, he was dismembered between four oxen in the city's main square – but luckily for us, his painting was smuggled out, and it clearly shows that group of robed figures some way over on the *right*-hand edge of the visible hemisphere, while the most prominent image in view is a strikingly large and complex flower-like design on the leftward side which was completely invisible in my time, though still spoken of longingly by the members of an Anticlockwiser faction who called themselves the Lotus People. Yet, interestingly, in Merccini's day, just as in mine and Meuli's, the Achieved Perfectionists were the dominant group, insisting that what was currently revealed of the Sphere contained its truest and most vital messages, and that what was hidden deserved to remain unseen.

My stay in the city was more than a quarter of a century ago, though, and the city has since then become part of the modern world. After a long period of negotiation, a reforming administration has installed a powerful electric motor which slowly turns the sphere so that it completes an entire revolution in a week. (In the deal struck between the various factions, it was agreed that it would turn clockwise in even years and anticlockwise in odd ones). Nothing is concealed any more, and only moderate persistence is required on the part of the visitor to view every part of the Sphere.

What is more, the ban on reproductions of the Sphere has also been lifted. Photography is still prohibited for copyright reasons, but it has now become possible to view every image and hieroglyph, simply by buying guidebooks or DVDs. Also available for sale these days, as I hardly need tell you, are those now ubiquitous revolving globes which can be found on so many mantelpieces, alongside Eiffel Towers, Big Bens and Spanish bulls. My great-aunt spent a weekend in the city with her friend Gill only last year, and acquired a large and rather expensive one with an interior light and its own electric motor.

Not surprisingly, since there is no longer any part of the Sphere that is lost or hidden, all the various factions of Clockwisers and Anticlockwisers have pretty much faded away, having lost the reason for their existence, while the modern heirs of the Achieved Perfectionists claim to have finally achieved a *truly* permanent settlement which accommodates every-one and excludes no one at all.

Curiously enough, though, the resolution of this ancient quarrel has led to a general loss of interest in the Sphere itself. I'm told that the only citizens of the city ever to be seen in front of it these days are tourist guides and souvenir sellers, and that, among the younger generation, the ability to read those strange and intricate hieroglyphs has now almost completely died out.

The Man Who
Swallowed Himself

'The poor guy's a victim of emotional abuse,' said Tim's friend Peter to his wife Sue, as they sat on their sofa watching TV. 'He can't do anything without her criticising him.'

Sue didn't agree.

'Well, it's his own fault,' she said. 'It's too easy to paint a woman like Mary as some sort of harridan. She makes demands of Tim, yes, like I do of you and you of me, but she meets no resistance.'

'Okay. So she gets exactly what she wants.'

'She doesn't, though. She doesn't at all. Because resistance itself is one of the things she's seeking. It's like a child behaving badly as a way of finding the boundaries that will keep her safe. Not that Mary's a child, I don't mean that at all, but we all need those boundaries. You and me provide them for one another. We both know the limits of what the other will tolerate, and it makes us feel safe.'

Peter considered this for some time.

'I guess you're right. That's interesting. I've never looked at it like that before. I mean, obviously I know that if I behave in certain kinds of ways you won't put up with it, but it hadn't occurred to me before that I actually need that from you. You're right, though, I do.'

'Well, it's the same with me. Remember how I used to fly into a tantrum sometimes, all those years ago, when things didn't go as I wanted? You just wouldn't play along with it, would you? You just ignored me completely till I pulled myself together. So I stopped, didn't I? And a good job too. You helped me to grow up.'

'I guess if I'd have been someone like Tim I would have run around in a panic, desperately trying to figure out what I had to do to placate you.'

'Exactly. And if *I'd* been someone like Tim, I'd have done the same when you went into one of those week-long sulks you used to go in for.'

Peter nodded.

'Tim can be *very* passive,' he conceded. 'He's like that at work as well. Dick treated him appallingly in a meeting the other day. I mean *really* appallingly. We all looked round at Tim, waiting for him to react – I mean it's not like Dick is even his boss or anything – but Tim didn't say anything at all. Not a word. He just looked down at his hands, and kind of… *swallowed.*'

'Swallowed? That's interesting. I've seen him do that too.'

'He always does it when Mary has a go at him. You remember that time at the Gibsons' party, for instance? Okay, I take your point, it may well be his own fault, but all the same, she really did humiliate him, dressing him down like a naughty child in front of everyone. And he just swallowed.'

'Yes, and remember when we went to Tenerife with them,' Sue said, 'and that guy in the market blatantly ripped him off. You wait for him to react, but he just—'

'—swallows. You can see his Adam's apple move. You can almost hear the gulp. Pathetic really.'

'And he's so *big*. That's the weird part. The tallest man we know, the broadest across the shoulders, a great big guy. He's like a bear that thinks it's a mouse.'

Peter laughed. 'I do like him, though, for some reason.'

'I quite like him too, though I often want to pick him up and shake him. I guess there's a reason he is as he is. I just don't accept that Mary made him that way.'

She watched the faces on the TV screen.

'Of course,' she said, 'he's absolutely full of rage.'

Peter looked round at her in surprise. 'Who? *Tim?* Are you mixing him up with someone else? The man hasn't got an angry bone in his body! That's his whole problem, surely?'

'I have this pain inside me,' Tim said, running his hand through his sandy-coloured hair. 'Well, it's more like a *pressure* really. Like something inside me squirming around and pushing outwards. It's probably stupid of me, but I can't help worrying that it's cancer or something like that. It feels a bit that way. It feels like some kind of alien force deep down in… well, I don't know where exactly, but somewhere right deep down in the core of me.'

The doctor laughed.

'Sounds like indigestion to me, Tim.'

He was a new doctor, fresh out of medical school, and he'd never met Tim before, but for some reason he thought it was okay to use the short form of Tim's first name, and to talk to him as if he was a child.

Tim swallowed. 'Well, I think I know what indigestion's like, actually. You could be right, I suppose, but it doesn't feel like that at all.'

'I'm sure you're fine.' The doctor had already turned to his keyboard. 'But I'll refer you for some tests for your own peace of mind. And meanwhile I'll prescribe you some antacid pills and we'll see if they're any help.'

It was growing inside him and it felt alive. It was as if there was a living animal trapped in there, struggling to free itself. And not just an animal, but a dangerous one, he was quite sure of that. He knew he must contain it, however difficult that might be.

'The doctor said it was just indigestion,' he told Mary as he came into the kitchen. 'He's given me some tablets for stomach acid.'

Little Sean was already at the table, waiting for his tea. He was five years old.

'Well, I told you it was nothing, didn't I?' Mary said. 'You don't need a doctor, Tim, you really don't, but if you carry on like this, you're going to need a shrink.'

'What's a shrink?' asked Sean.

'Hello there, my little man,' said Tim, kissing the boy's head as he sat down at the table.

He loved his son with such intensity that sometimes it felt to him as if a dazzling light was blazing outwards from the little boy, almost too bright to look at.

'A shrink is someone you go to when your suit's too tight,' Mary said.

She meant it to be a joke of course but, funnily enough, it wasn't a bad description of what his symptoms actually felt like.

'Really?' Sean asked doubtfully.

'Well, sort of,' Tim said, 'except that I feel like the suit.'

Sean looked worried.

'No, not really, Sean,' Tim told his son, squeezing his hand. 'Your mum was only kidding. She means your dad is making a big fuss about nothing, and she's probably right.'

He glanced at Mary, and she gave him a thin taut smile as she laid out the sausages and mash. Later he would read Sean his bedtime story and then the little boy, already half asleep, would reach up his arms and plant a soft wet kiss on his mouth.

'Goodnight, my little man,' Tim would say, as he

tiptoed out, leaving his son to the protection of the plastic lion that always kept watch on his bedside table.

'You're quite right, of course,' he said to Mary later, when they were lying in bed. 'I must stop worrying about it so much.'

'You really must,' she said, turning the page of her book. 'It's one of those silly things that feed on themselves. You're a bit prone to those, aren't you? You've let this blow up out of all proportion.'

'I have,' he admitted. 'I'm glad about the tests, though. Let's hope when they come back, I'll be able to lay the whole thing to rest.'

He glanced across at her. She looked very appealing with her low-cut nightdress showing a great deal of those shapely breasts that were beginning to swell and fill with pregnancy.

'I don't suppose you...?'

'Not tonight, Tim. It's been a long day, and I need to get some sleep.'

Tim nodded.

'Sure,' he said. 'That's absolutely fine. Only it's been quite a while.'

Tim swallowed. Mary turned out the light.

Suddenly he saw the creature vividly in his mind. It was bloody and red, with fierce, burning eyes. He knew it would terrify Sean if he ever saw it. He knew it would tear their little home apart. So one thing at least was absolutely clear: whatever happened, whether the symptoms could be alleviated or not, he must keep that thing locked away inside himself, he must never never—

But now, lying there in the dark, Tim checked himself. These were mad thoughts, surely? Either this was an illness of some kind, like indigestion, or, more likely, it was something in his head, like that time he became convinced that there was a gas leak, even though Mary couldn't smell anything, and even though the guy from the gas company came out twice and found no trace at all. An illness, or something in his head: it was one of those two. He must stop thinking of it as some kind of living thing.

'He shouldn't have spoken to me like that, though,' he muttered, thinking about the young doctor and his patronising tone.

A spark of anger appeared in his mind, apparently from nowhere. It was as if he was looking at a fireplace sideways from across a room. He couldn't see the grate, he couldn't see the fire itself, but he could see the red hot fragment as it jumped out onto the floor.

He swallowed again.

'I'm actually getting quite worried about Tim,' Peter said to his wife. 'He looks *so* distracted these days.'

They were washing the dishes together. She was drying. Outside the window, rain was falling into their patio from a heavy dark grey sky.

'Hasn't he always looked like that? I often get the

feeling with Tim that he's not really there at all. He's somewhere far away, operating his body with some difficulty by remote control, while simultaneously dealing with something else entirely that none of us can see.'

Peter laughed. 'That's a bit harsh!'

She picked up a wet saucepan from the drying rack.

'I'm not criticising him, I'm just telling you how I see him. Like he's never quite learnt how to inhabit himself.'

'Maybe,' said Peter. 'But there's something else going on for him now. Some new thing. Sometimes, when he doesn't know I'm looking, I see him wincing like he's in pain.'

'Well, maybe he is.'

'He did say something about going to the doctor a couple of weeks ago. Something about stomach problems. But when I asked him how he got on, he just laughed and said it had turned out to be nothing. "Possibly indigestion," he said, "but probably just hypochondria." Something's eating him, though, Sue. It's obvious. Something's really eating him. He's not right at all.'

Peter's wife put down the now-dry saucepan and picked up a dripping casserole.

'Well, what else can you do about it?' she asked. 'It sounds like you've offered him plenty of chances to talk. I'm not sure there's much more you can contribute, apart from doing the same from time to time.'

'Tim's on his own for a week, as of today. Mary and Sean have gone to stay with her mum in Gloucester so he can get on with some decorating before the new baby comes. I said I'd call him and take him out for a drink. Okay, I appreciate it may be his fault as much as hers but, rightly or wrongly, Mary really does scare the life out of him. I thought he might feel able to talk more freely when she was out of the picture.'

'Good idea.'

Peter's wife laid down the casserole and kissed him on the cheek.

'I know Tim's a bit of a drip in many ways,' Peter said, 'but I do like him. There's more to him than meets the eye. There are layers to him.'

'I agree,' she said. And then, picking up a wet plate: 'It's not just Mary he's frightened of, is it? It's everyone. The only person in the world he really feels safe with is that little boy of his.'

'Well, it would be hard to deal with other people, if you had to operate your body by remote control. Imagine how stressful it would be.'

'God, will you look at this rain!' Sue said. 'I'm glad we live on a hill.'

The tests had come back negative.

'There's nothing inside you that shouldn't be, Tim,' the doctor had said with a laugh.

But there it was anyway, pressing imperiously outwards, prodding and clamouring for his attention.

He piled books into boxes in the back bedroom and lugged the full boxes out onto the landing. He rolled up the carpet, carried out all the furniture that he could easily move on his own, and then dragged the bed away from the wall and threw a dustsheet over it. It had been the spare bedroom since they moved in, but now it was going to be Sean's. The new baby would have the middle room.

Tim doused the walls in paper stripper, and then went downstairs for a mug of tea while it soaked in. As he was pouring in the milk, the phone began to ring. He could see on the phone's little screen that it was Peter calling, his good friend Peter, probably his best friend, ringing no doubt to arrange the drink he'd suggested earlier in the week. But Tim didn't pick up. He just stood there in the kitchen with the mug in his hand, watching the phone ring and ring, and feeling the eerie presence of another mind reaching towards him, unable to see him, but prodding and poking into his house as it blindly sought him out. It was hard to believe, really, that Peter couldn't sense him here, right beside the ringing phone. Tim backed away from it, as if into the shadows.

Ten times the phone rang. And then suddenly it stopped. There was complete silence. No one was near him any more. The probe had withdrawn. The other mind had pulled back, and was once again a whole mile away across the city, turning its attention to other things.

'I'll call him back tomorrow,' Tim said.

He went back upstairs and began to attack the walls. The blade slid easily between the liner and the plaster beneath, right up to the handle, and he pulled away a long and satisfying strip and tossed it behind him onto the floor. It was like pulling off a scab from a large but well-healed wound. Soon he'd established a rhythm, working so fast and hard that he was able to forget all his worries, including the creature inside him.

About halfway along the wall he uncovered a scrawl in his own writing on the bare plaster.

'Help!' it said, and there was a little cartoon face beneath it, with its mouth open, like that famous painting *The Scream*.

He usually wrote or drew random things on walls before he papered or painted them. Secrets and hiding places had always appealed to him: time capsules, hidden rooms, magic wardrobes. Every room in the house had one or more of these messages, all of them intended to be funny or surreal, so perhaps it wasn't all that surprising he had no particular recollection of writing this one. But it felt very strange to uncover this evidence of another Tim, thinking and acting in a moment that the present Tim no longer had any connection with. It was like that thing that sometimes happened on car journeys, when he'd suddenly realise he had no memory of the last ten miles. Clearly someone had been conscious and driving the car because here he was, having apparently successfully negotiated two roundabouts and a busy T-junction, and no doubt the someone who'd accomplished all of that would have considered himself to be Tim. But this Tim had no memory of that one, and of course that Tim had had no memory of a Tim who, at the time, had not yet even come into being. So in what sense could they be said to be one and the same person?

Outside the window rain was falling steadily, pattering on the glass, gurgling down pipes and into drains, battering against wet leaves.

Tim fetched a pencil, and added more words to the message on the wall.

'Help! Missing self. Answers to the name of Tim. £50 reward for information leading to its safe return.'

All that night the rain kept up, and on into the next day. In the lower parts of the city drains overflowed, and rivers and streams, long buried under tarmac and concrete, rose from their hidden conduits and began running down the streets. Some people put sandbags outside their front doors, or moved their best furniture in case of floods. It was all very exciting. The local news was full of it.

The following morning was a Saturday, and Peter and his wife stayed home, sitting companionably side by side on their living room sofa with the radio on, while they caught up on emails and paperwork that they'd been putting off: a bill to pay, a letter to answer, a car insurance document to file. Several times, Peter picked up his phone and tried to call his friend but the phone just rang and rang.

'What's the matter, I wonder? Why won't he pick up?'

'Well, he's decorating, isn't he?' his wife said. 'He'll be all covered with paint or something, and he doesn't want to have to keep stopping and coming to the phone. You're probably driving him nuts with all your ringing.'

'I'm not sure. I've sent him a couple of texts and he hasn't replied to them either. I feel he's hiding from me. I think he does that sometimes, hides away, when the one thing he most needs is to get out and be with other people.'

Tim slept very badly that night, woken again and again by the pressure inside himself, and at 6 a.m. he finally gave up on the hope of more rest, made himself coffee, and began to put up the new paper in Sean's room. Sean had chosen it himself from a catalogue. It had a design of railway tracks and trains with cheerful drivers and passengers smiling and waving out of the windows. By 10.30 Tim had papered over his pencilled message, and by midday he'd completed the whole room. Before he went down to eat, he moved all Sean's things back into it, made up the bed with the train-themed covers they'd bought to match the wallpaper, and carefully replaced Sean's plastic lion on the bedside table.

'He'll love this,' Tim said to himself, as he stood

back and admired the overall effect. He could hardly wait to show it to his boy.

Then a sharp stab of pain made him gasp.

Damn that doctor! That *hurt*! This was *way* too raw and crude and physical to just be a trick of the mind! There was something in there, something solid and real.

But then a new and disturbing thought came to him. If there really *was* something in there, then perhaps there was no choice about it? Perhaps it *had* to come out?

Mary was not a coward and she wasn't at all given to self-pity, but at the beginning of her labour with Sean, she'd quailed for a short while as she realised just what an assault on her body this was going to be. The antenatal classes had taught her all sorts of sensible and useful things, but they hadn't prepared her at all for the sheer primal violence of the process, the utter indifference that nature showed towards the individual creatures that were its instruments. The classes had been warm and reassuring. They hadn't really engaged with the fact that, through most of history, and still through much of the world, labour was a time of acute jeopardy, a time when mother or baby or both were at serious risk of death.

'I can't do this,' she'd whimpered to Tim. 'I just can't do this.'

But of course she'd had no choice. You might as well ask a hurricane to take a different route, or a river to flow back uphill. The baby must come out of her, alive or dead, if she herself was going to survive.

And quickly seeing this, Mary had taken a grip on herself, set her brief moment of funk behind her, and begun to push.

'No!' Tim muttered, as he started draping sheets over the furniture in the living room. 'That's stupid. There's no comparison at all.'

The living room was second on the to-do list that Mary had prepared for him.

'For one thing there's no danger to me,' he pointed out as he mixed up wallpaper stripper in a bucket. 'The doctor said so, and the tests backed him up. Whatever this is, it isn't a threat to my life.'

But the creature inside him wasn't listening. It gave a violent shove that made him yelp out loud. And at that moment, the phone began to ring yet again, probing into the house with its blind insistent fingers.

'For Christ's sake, give it a rest!' Tim screamed at it. 'Why can't you just leave me alone? I don't need you to deal with as well. I don't need you and your bloody friendship.'

'He's still not picking up,' Peter said. 'I'm actually quite worried now. I think I'll stroll over there after tea.'

His wife was lying with her head in his lap, half-watching TV and half-sleeping.

'In *this* rain? I wouldn't call that a stroll!'

'Well, I do own a raincoat, Sue,' he pointed out. 'And it's less than a mile away. I'll enjoy the rest of the evening more if I've seen he's alright and arranged a time to meet with him.'

Tim scraped away at the living room wall so hard and so fast that he had to strip to the waist to keep cool. Covered in sweat, with aching arms and a pounding heart, he attacked the paper, he ripped it apart, he assaulted it, but all the while he was really fighting the creature inside himself. It must *not* come out! Nothing could be allowed to threaten the warm nest that he and Mary had made for the little boy that Tim loved far more than he loved himself, and for the new baby that he would love in the same way. It must stay inside him!

But a time came when he just couldn't concentrate any more on scraping. He was exhausted for one thing – he'd reached a point where he had to keep pausing just to catch his breath and let his heart rate slow – but, more than that, he was finding that, however vigorously he worked, the job was still too static to be bearable in his present state of mind. He needed to move. He couldn't bear to be in one place. Clutching the scraper in his hand, he began to roam the house, restlessly prowling upstairs and downstairs and from room to room, muttering and groaning, kicking at skirting boards from time to time, pounding his fist on the walls.

It was in Sean's new room, as it turned out, the one with the happy trains on the walls and the lion on the bedside table, that he finally realised he'd lost the battle.

'It just *has* to come out,' he whispered. 'I can't hold it in any more.'

He had no more choice than Mary had had in that room in the maternity suite. No matter how many machines were humming around her, how many tubes and wires were attached to her, how many dispassionate little green graphs were tracking the rhythms of her body, the basic fact remained that the baby inside her would have to emerge in one way or another.

And now a strange thing happened, which he hadn't anticipated at all. As he finally gave way to the brute reality which he'd been fighting for so long, he discovered that he wasn't pushing *in* any more, but pushing out. It was as if the rules of the game had been reversed. Having abandoned the project of keeping the alien creature inside himself, he was noticing the rigid cage that held it in. Up to now this cage had simply been *himself*, the real Tim, its rigidity the expression of his own will, the measure of his own determination to contain the threat. He'd even taken a certain pride in its firmness. He knew perfectly well that others saw him as unassertive and weak, but that rigid cage had proved to him that he was stronger than they knew, brave in a way they couldn't see.

But now, quite suddenly, he was experiencing that cage as an alien presence, a hard unyielding obstacle that was constricting and stifling him, denying him movement, limiting his access to light and air, standing between him and the world. Only a few seconds ago he would have called that cage himself, but it *wasn't* him. It was the *opposite* of him. It was the thing that had imprisoned him all his life.

'Let me out, fuck you,' he heard his own voice screaming at it. 'Let me out, you bastard, and let me breathe.'

After that he stopped using words. He just bellowed and roared and punched the walls, like a boxer pumping himself up before a fight, building up immunity to pain and fear.

Rain beat down on the roofs and pavements, and onto the doorsteps, and into the hedges and the little front gardens. The few cars that were out crept slowly along with their headlights on, their wipers flinging out great wet dollops with every sweep. Lights were switched on inside the houses, curtains drawn. No one but Peter was out on foot.

When he reached Tim's house, he found the front door wide open, with rain blowing in, and the doormat sitting in a pool of water. All the lights were turned on, but when he called Tim's name there was no answer. Peter stepped inside, throwing back the hood of his raincoat.

He found one of the living room walls stripped

down, and half of another, furniture clumped in the middle of the room under sheets, and old wallpaper lying on the floor in twisted heaps. There was even a swathe of paper dangling from the wall, as if Tim had stopped in mid-scrape. Peter looked into the kitchen and the downstairs toilet. He saw a couple of teacups waiting to be washed, a dirty plate, a paint-brush set to soak in a bucket of water.

'Tim?' he called. 'Are you there?'

Tim could have fallen from a ladder or some-thing, Peter had been thinking as he'd walked over from his house. He could have knocked himself out, or broken a bone and been unable to get to the phone. But if so, where was he now? The living room was obviously what he'd been working on. If he'd had a fall, wouldn't it have been in there?

Then Peter noticed something that he hadn't spotted when he first came in. There were red marks on the stairs. Perhaps Tim had cut himself somehow and gone up to the bathroom to dress the wound. He could have passed out from loss of blood.

'Tim? It's Peter! Are you alright?'

There was nothing unusual in the bathroom, though, or in the front bedroom, or the middle room which, as Tim had told him, was going to be the baby's.

'Tim?'

The door of the back bedroom was ajar and the light inside was on, as all the lights had been, all round the house.

'Tim, are you in there?'

Another possibility occurred to Peter. Perhaps there'd been a break-in. Perhaps there was a stranger in there, holding a knife to Tim's throat, or even crouching in readiness beside Tim's corpse. He picked up a hammer that had been propped against the landing wall, and, clutching it firmly, advanced into the little boy's new room.

'Tim? Are you—?'

Peter broke off. There was no one in there, alive or dead, but, strewn right across the room were bloody flaps of skin and hunks of sandy-coloured hair. Dark red strips were scattered over the bed and the chest of drawers. Congealing fragments clung to the walls, with red trails above them to indicate how far they'd slid downwards since they were first splattered over those cheerful little trains. A single narrow shred of skin was draped over the lion on the bedside table.

The scraper lay in the middle of the floor, with dark blood clinging to its blade and handle. But there was no Tim. Whatever had happened here, Tim had gone.

The Gates of Eden

I made a mistake at work. I got a large order completely wrong, costing the company a great deal of
money, and losing us a particularly valuable cus-
tomer at a difficult time when our profit margins
were at rock bottom and we were struggling to
keep our market share. There was no real excuse
for my blunder, and, as often seems to happen, I
compounded my original mistake by making other
secondary errors as I struggled to put things right.

I'd been summoned to Head Office down in
Bournemouth to explain myself. There was a very
good chance of losing my job and I was terrified. I'd
been part of the sales force of this same company
for over twenty years. I knew I wasn't as sharp and
energetic as I once had been, and that my value to
the company, such as it was, lay in my knowledge of
the company itself and the people it dealt with. I very
much doubted I could find another job on anything
like the same money, or even another job at all, but
I had a big mortgage to pay and two teenaged kids,
who I'd brought up by myself since their father's
death ten years previously.

'You're amazing, Jenny,' my friends used to say to me back in those early years. 'Full time work, kids, all by yourself. None of us know how you hold it all together. We know we couldn't.' I'd brush this off, as you do – 'Nonsense, you'd do exactly the same as me if you had to. I just didn't have a choice' – but actually it had been very important to me, and a source of great pride. I felt bitterly ashamed that I'd not lived up to it, and at the same time I felt resentful, because actually, whatever I said to my friends, most people *couldn't* do what I had done, most people would have stumbled, and that being so, it seemed very unfair that I should have this shame to deal with, and they should not. Most of all, though, I felt afraid: afraid of what faced me in Bournemouth, and afraid of what lay beyond: telling the kids that we'd have to move somewhere smaller, for instance, stirring up memories of that old catastrophe of their dad's suicide.

It was a beautiful September day when I drove down, with air as clear as newly cleaned glass, achingly blue sky, and trees just lightly brushed with gold, but I saw all of this through a complicated cage of painful feelings which had the effect of setting it beyond my reach and denying me the solace it might have given me, just when I needed it most. I was terrified of being told off. I was dreading the humiliation of being cross-examined and found incompetent or unprofessional, after so long in the job. I worried that perhaps I never really *had* been any good at this job I'd done all these years, and that my bluff had finally been called. I rehearsed every small mistake I'd ever made, every embarrassing gaffe. And over and over again, I imagined having to tell the kids that the life I'd given them was going to have to be dismantled. Without the job, we couldn't keep the house. We couldn't even live in the same area.

Worry comes readily to me. I can put on a good impression of being calm and unflappable but the truth is that, even on an ordinary day, there are always a lot of things niggling away inside me, and I often find it hard to sleep. I guess when your husband suddenly kills himself, it does sap your confidence in your ability to control events. But actually I think I'd always been the worrying kind, even as a kid, and there were plenty of more recent things to worry about: Ben's difficulties at school, for one, and my friend Carrie's cancer, and my relationship with Harry that hovered all the time between being on and being off, and never quite settled either way. I worried a lot, but it was bad this time. This was the bedrock of everything that was under threat, and as I drove through the New Forest, I felt quite sick with fear.

All around me, the warmth of the sun was making the heather steam. A herd of deer were grazing peacefully by a stream. But that was out there. That was for the happy people. It gave me no pleasure at all, no respite. It had nothing to do with me.

·

As I do when I'm anxious about a meeting, I'd set off ridiculously early so as to be absolutely sure of not arriving late. As a result, when I reached the far side of the forest, I realised I was only twelve miles from my destination with nearly two hours to fill before the meeting. To kill some time I pulled over at a Little Chef place, sat at a window table, and, after ordering a coffee, began to read through, yet one more time, the various papers that I'd brought with me: the documents from HR, my own statement setting out the somewhat flimsy extenuating circumstances I'd been able to scrape together, and a list I'd compiled of some of the important contracts I'd secured for our company over the years, by way of demonstrating that there was a positive side to my balance sheet.

When the coffee arrived, I took a sip and, for a while, carried on looking through the papers. But I was getting quite panicky now. I really wasn't taking in what I was reading, and I realised I'd just get myself into even more of a muddle if I went over it any more. So I pushed the papers away and took another sip of my coffee. I'd barely noticed the first sip, but second time round I felt the warm buzz as the caffeine entered my bloodstream.

I put the mug down again and, as I did so, I noticed how the steam rising up from it caught the sunbeams streaming in through the window beside me, and it suddenly struck me that the sunbeams and the steam each made the other visible. I was sufficiently intrigued by this, that I began to experiment. When the steam rose through them, the parallel sunbeams that were revealed were as firm and steady as bars of metal, but if I gently blew the steam away, they disappeared completely into empty air, only to reappear when I stopped blowing and let the steam rise from the mug once more. I blew again, very gently – it only took the smallest puff – and watched the steam and the sunbeams vanish again, and then rapidly reassert themselves as the temporary agitation I'd created settled down. I stopped interfering after that, and just sat and watched the play of steam and light over my coffee, enjoying the sensation of the sun warming my skin as I sat by the window with the bright world outside. It was several minutes before I noticed I was completely at peace.

At *peace*? Me? Surely not! But I prodded my feelings carefully, and it really seemed to be the case. The things I'd been worrying about hadn't vanished, the dreaded meeting still lay ahead of me, the future was still full of uncertainty and threats to myself and the ones I loved, but even so, right then, I felt entirely content. It may seem an odd thing to say, but it was as if I'd suddenly remembered an ancient deal that was the basis of my existence, and could see that it was necessary and fair. You can have no mind at all and be completely at peace, as sunlight is, or steam, and that's always an option, as my husband Dick proved: you can always revert to being inanimate matter. Or you can have a mind that knows it's alive and is capable of pleasure and delight. But if you choose the latter, you have to pay the necessary price for it in vigilance and worry and suffering. No one can live in the Garden of Eden, even though it's where we come from and where we'll return. That's why it's so peaceful.

Of course, there is only so much time you can spend watching steam and sunbeams and thinking profound thoughts. After a time, I got out my tablet and occupied myself with emails until it was time to go. I still felt quite cheerful, though, and, as I drove off I decided that, if I ever took it into my head to found a religion – if religions are ever founded by middle-aged sales managers with two kids and a boyfriend who won't quite commit himself – the Little Chef restaurant on the A338 would definitely be one of its holiest shrines. People would come on pilgrimages there, so as to stare at the spot where the prophet Jenny experienced enlightenment. The area round the window would be roped off to ensure no one could sully the holy Formica table, or steal the sacred sauce bottle. The blessed laminated menu would have to be chained down.

None of those pilgrims would experience what I'd experienced, though. Not in there. Not with pilgrims and tourists pushing and shoving for a view under the watchful and suspicious eyes of the official guardians of the shrine: 'No photography please. You can buy a picture in the shop, if you want one!'

But the funny thing was that they'd experience similar peaceful moments at other times and in other places, maybe even quite frequently, and yet barely even noticed them. And so they'd still keep coming to look at the sacred sauce bottle in the hope of some kind of salvation.

I was quite entertained for a while by these thoughts. I even imagined a Great Schism, when two rival Jennyist churches would fight for control of the Little Chef, while members of a small breakaway group insisted that the moment of enlightenment had actually occurred in the Burger King down the road. Next thing they'd be burning folk at the stake for denying that the beverage I drank here had, in some wonderful and inexplicable way, been quite literally transformed as it touched my lips, so that it ceased to be mere Little Chef coffee and became the elixir of eternal life. And then, of course…

But now worry was starting to intrude again. I would soon be at company headquarters, parking my car, checking my hair and makeup, and gathering my things together for that lonely walk to reception and the dreaded waiting area. I'd had my interlude of peace, and now I had to deal with a threat to the conditions of my existence, as living creatures must. Fear began to gnaw inside me as I approached the outskirts of Bournemouth.

As it turned out, the meeting didn't go anything like as badly as I'd thought it would. My argument about all the business I'd brought in proved to be more persuasive than I'd dared to hope. We agreed that I had indeed made a very bad and costly mistake, but it wasn't characteristic of me, and I'd contributed a good deal to the fact that our company was still afloat at all, in a difficult market, with new global competitors emerging all the time. We decided that I still had a lot to offer, but that perhaps my moment of carelessness was a sign that I needed a change. A different role was suggested to me, a more strategic role, but on the same pay as I was receiving now. There were still Ben's problems at school to worry about, there was still Carrie's possible cancer and all the clumsy heartache of my relationship with Harry. There was still the distinct possibility that the company itself would founder. But one threat, at least for the moment, had been warded off.

The sky had clouded over a bit by the time I headed for home, as is often the case on autumn days which start out sunny. As I drove back up the A338, I passed the place where I'd stopped for coffee, but it was just an ordinary Little Chef now, like all the others, with the usual angel standing guard outside it, wielding a sword of fire.

Aphrodite

There was a sea running east to west between two big brown bodies of land. In the eastern part of the sea there were many islands, and among them one island in particular that was long and thin in shape. At one end of this island a holiday resort had grown up, with bright lights, discos, rows of restaurants and music thumping till dawn, at the other there was a village falling into decline at the foot of an extinct volcano.

Thomas, who was going through a somewhat difficult time, had gone to the resort at first but was now in the village, eating a salad of tomatoes and goat cheese by himself, outside the small café where he'd rented a room, a place that also doubled as a general store. As Thomas munched, the big plane tree in the middle of the square was throwing long and somehow dreary shadows towards him over the cracked and oil-stained tarmac to remind him that the day was ending and the streets of this very quiet village would soon be empty and dark. A stooped old woman in black turned to stare at him as she hobbled past. He smiled and raised his hand in greeting, but her cold appraisal didn't so much as flicker. This was not a welcoming place. Apart from one other, smaller café, there was nowhere else in it that he could go, and many of the houses were empty and boarded up. As the café proprietor replaced the empty bread basket with a full one on the chequered plastic tablecloth in front of him, a worm of doubt stirred in Thomas's mind. Had it been a bad decision, coming here? Wasn't he going to have a very dull and very lonely week?

'There was an Irish woman here earlier, a young woman about your age,' his host said. '*Very* pretty. She had arranged to meet some friends here for camping, but they missed their flight. It will be a couple of days before they join her, apparently. I offered her a room, but...' he paused to give a comically bewildered shrug, 'but she said she was going to sleep outside.'

His name was Spiro and his rugged face kept reminding Thomas of a gone-to-seed version of Zorba the Greek, as played by Anthony Quinn. Thomas suspected that Spiro was well aware of the Anglo-Saxon stereotype of the earthy, sensual Mediterranean man, and consciously played the part: a Greek playing a Mexican actor playing a Greek. But then again Thomas knew that, when the worm stirred inside him, it always made him ungenerous and a little paranoid.

'There's a temple here, isn't there? A ruined temple? I thought I'd go and look at it before the light goes.'

'The temple of Aphrodite,' Spiro winked broadly, 'the goddess of love. It's about two kilometres away, along that track just there.'

The track led through a dry, open forest of pine trees and wiry scrub, the warm air heavy with resin and pulsating with the constant shrill scraping of millions of cicadas. After an outcrop of bare grey rock the track dipped down, and a side path branched off from it along a small wooded valley towards the sea. There was a clifftop down there, he knew, and below it a beach, which you could also access directly via a path from the village. But for now Thomas stayed on the main track as it climbed up again, past a metal shrine that smelled of honey, and began to skirt round the broad shoulder of that extinct volcano.

The temple stood on a kind of terrace on the right-hand side of the track, with the wooded slope beyond it leading down to cliffs above the sea. There wasn't much left of the building itself, just a stone floor, the bases of the columns round the edge, and on the near side, a couple of broken columns that still rose about a metre from the ground. In front of it was a rusty sign with an empty beer bottle at its foot. The sun was almost at the horizon, and a pathway of yellow light stretched across the sea towards the island. All around, in every direction, the cicadas kept beating out their unrelenting rhythm, like a million children shaking dried peas in yoghurt pots.

Thomas sat on a piece of fallen column that lay a few yards on from the temple itself. The light faded much more quickly here than it would have done back at home, and in a short time, a warm, scented darkness had closed round him. But more light was on its way. The sea along the horizon was already silvery with moonlight and soon the moon had risen high enough above the mountain behind him to illuminate the temple's broken columns, cast faint shadows over its pale floor, and transform the forest around it into a kind of stage set: empty still, but full of dimly lit places where characters would meet, and shadows where they would hide. Thomas noticed that he no longer felt that worm of doubt inside him. This was the world and he was in it. And that, for the moment, was enough.

Then he noticed he wasn't alone. Someone else had stepped out onto the stage, coming from the direction of the village. To begin with the stranger was merely a pattern in the patchwork of shadow and dim light, distinguishable from the rest only because it moved. He couldn't see a face, or make out the colour of the clothes, but quite soon he could tell somehow that this was a woman, and he sat and watched as she took form, knowing that he himself would be invisible as long as he stayed where he was. In fact, she still hadn't spotted him even when she stepped onto the floor of the temple, but he could see that she was about his own age, slender, athletic, and wearing the clothes of a tourist like himself, and he assumed she was the Irishwoman that Spiro had told him about. Perhaps the old Greek had pointed her this way.

'Hi there,' he called out, standing up. He'd been reluctant to separate himself from the shadows, but to hide any longer would just be creepy.

'Oh hi. Jesus, you made me jump! I thought I was on my own.'

Yes, she was certainly Irish.

'Sorry, I should have spoken sooner.' He walked towards her, stepping up onto the floor of the temple, worn shiny by two and a half millennia of feet.

They were standing beside one of the broken columns now: man and woman, dimly lit in shades of grey. There was no black or white. Everything was provisional, everything on the point of dissolution.

'I'm Siobhan. You're must be the Englishman the café guy mentioned.'

She reached out her hand. Their palms and fingers touched, suddenly firm and solid, and she looked up into his face with friendly but appraising eyes. He wondered if she was as aware as he was of the obvious narrative which the universe, perhaps with Spiro's assistance, had set up for them.

So where did you two first meet?

Would you believe it, we met by moonlight in the Temple of the Goddess of Love.

'Hi, I'm Thomas. I gather your friends have been held up?'

'Yes, a couple of days.'

'And you're sleeping out in the open?'

'I am. The others have got the tent.'

'Are you short of money until your friends come? If so I could easily—'

'I'm fine. It's no hardship sleeping out when the nights are as warm as this.'

'I guess not. I just wondered whether there was a problem because your—'

'There's no problem at all. And I'm looking forward to a couple of days by myself if I'm honest. I like being on my own.'

Thomas nodded.

'Me too.'

He did like it, actually, if he was in the right frame of mind, but that was something he'd only recently learnt about himself, as he grew older and became very gradually better at separating out the question 'what do I want?' from 'what, right at this moment, would be the easiest thing to do?' He'd lately discovered, for instance, that he didn't really enjoy staying up drinking until 4 in the morning, or hanging out in places where you couldn't talk but only bellow like a beast. This had been the cause of an ugly row with the friends who'd come with him to the resort at the far end of the island, and was the reason he was now here. It had all been rather unpleasant and, in retrospect, he could see he'd handled the whole thing very badly.

'There isn't much to do at this end of the island, is the only problem,' he said. 'The only things open in the village are Spiro's café, and one other café that looks like it's very much for locals only.'

'Yes, I know. I've kind of resigned myself to a very early bedtime. I'm hoping the journey will have worn me out enough to get me off to sleep.'

'Well, why not have a drink with me back at the village before you settle down?' would have been the obvious thing for Thomas to say at this point. It would have been a natural thing to do, in no way difficult or awkward, and certainly not pushy or overfamiliar. Arguably it would actually be rather unfriendly *not* to make the offer, given that it was very early in the evening to lie down to sleep, and Siobhan couldn't retreat to a room as he could, or read a book by electric light. And what was more, Thomas liked Siobhan immediately. Not only was she very pretty – Spiro was quite right about that – but she projected a kind of lively curiosity that he found instantly appealing. He liked the fact that she was Irish too, and different in that small way from himself.

But he didn't suggest a drink all the same.

'Well, nice to meet you, Siobhan. I've actually been here a while and I was just thinking of heading back.'

He was surprised at himself. He could already see, without even the benefit of hindsight, that this was going to be one of those moments he would replay in his mind. *I should never have walked away from that Irish girl*, he knew he'd tell himself at lonely moments, perhaps even years from now. Stupid, of course, but it would happen. And never mind the distant future. What about this very evening, what about the prospect ahead of him, trying to fill the time by himself in that sad little village? He *did* like being on his own, it was quite true, but there were places where that worked, and places where it didn't. A depressed and slowly dying village wasn't a good setting for solitude.

But still he walked away. The argument with his friends had shaken him quite badly. He'd been shocked by his own sudden eruption of rage. It had made him think about his dealings with other people in general, and the way he swung so suddenly from one feeling to another, from friendliness to contempt, from passion to indifference. And he was tired of blowing about in the wind, and doing whatever seemed easiest at the time. He knew he'd hurt people that way, especially women, and he'd had enough of the mess and shame when the wind suddenly changed.

As Siobhan watched him dissolve into the forest, she wondered why he'd been in such a hurry to get away. He'd seemed very reserved, even by English stand-ards, but she'd quite liked the look of him, and had assumed he'd like the look of her too – well, why wouldn't he? – enough in any case for an evening together to seem like a pleasant prospect. Perhaps he was just shy, she thought. Maybe she should have suggested it herself? But something had stopped her. Siobhan wasn't prone to shyness, so it wasn't that. No, it was almost as if he'd seen her thought and metaphorically held up a warning hand. Which was kind of odd.

But anyway, never mind. By the time she'd unwrapped the cheese and tomato sandwich that had travelled with her all the way from Dublin airport, she was enjoying the ruin in the moonlight and the chorus of cicadas, and thinking about other things. After about fifteen minutes, she headed back herself along the track.

When she reached the side path towards the sea, she paused. She could go straight on to the village now and, as likely as not, she'd meet Thomas again outside the café, for where else was there for him to go? She could stop for a word and, if he seemed more amenable this time, a companion for the evening would perhaps be an option once more. Or she could turn left now down the path towards her little camp on top of the cliff. Spending the night there had been quite appealing in prospect, even in the absence of the camping equipment that her friends were bringing, but it seemed rather less so now. Meeting Thomas, and then watching him go, had made her more aware of the fact that she was on her own, and she felt unnerved by the moonlit forest and its shadowy and ambiguous forms. But recognising this fact made up her mind for her. She didn't like to give way to unfounded fears. She preferred to push on through them.

She'd just turned down the little valley when she saw a man ahead of her, standing just a few yards back from the path, completely motionless, and watching her with an odd, sardonic, sideways gaze. This was genuinely frightening and she was on the point of turning back and heading for the village after all when she realised this wasn't a human being at all, but only the broken trunk of a tree. Amused by her own irrational fear, she walked over to the tree to give it a little kick, and had just returned to the path when suddenly a real man appeared on the path ahead with a gun in his hand, striding determinedly towards her. Her heart began to race again but the hunter walked straight past, heading back to the village without saying a word, and Siobhan was on her own again.

How different it seemed on the cliff now, in the dark. She searched for some time for the sleeping bag which she'd left in a small hollow under some rocks, cursing herself for not marking the spot more clearly, and worrying that perhaps it had been stolen. Eventually she found it, though, and this was immensely comforting, a moment in fact of really intense happiness. Even returning to a patch of earth on a clifftop, it seemed, could feel, in the right circumstances, like coming home. She knew she wouldn't sleep for some time, but she rolled out her sleeping bag and lay down quite contentedly on the outside of it. The stars were very bright, and the entire span of the Milky Way was stretched out above her across the sky. She wished she could name the constellations, but the only one she could remember was Orion, shining up there above the mountain.

Never mind. The stars didn't know their names.

Still awake an hour later, she stood up and stretched herself and, as she did so, she looked down over the side of her rocky hollow at the small beach beneath, its narrow strip of sand dimly visible in the moonlight, and little waves glowing softly as they broke over it. Some way out to sea, the lamps of several fishing boats were moving slowly across the water, the crouched fishermen inside them half in light and half in darkness.

She was watching their slow progress when she became aware of movement below her. There was a direct path to the beach from the village and a man was walking along it. She could see it was Thomas. Shadowy and indistinct as he was in the moonlight, there was something slightly dogged about his walk that she immediately recognised. It was as if he was battling against something, she thought, forcing himself forward into the world against some sort of resistance. She saw him pull off his T-shirt and shorts and wade out naked into the sea. The water glittered around him as he dived in, and it seemed a long time before he emerged again to swim thirty or forty strokes further out in a strong, confident crawl, before stopping and treading water so he could turn and look back at the shore. Not wanting him to see her watching him, Siobhan squatted down again behind her rocks.

Soon afterwards, she decided to get inside her sleeping bag, for the air was beginning to cool. As she lay there, she imagined herself in Thomas's place: the moonlight under the sea, the play of grey shadows on the blurry stones on the bottom, the coolness of the water against her skin. If they'd spent the evening together, she thought, the two of them might well have both come swimming. By then he'd no longer be the shadowy being she'd met at the temple in the moonlight. They would have talked for a while, seen each other's faces properly in electric light, knocked back a few glasses of beer or wine or ouzo or something, and learnt a few anchoring facts about one another, like where each of them came from, what they did for a living, and who was in their families. There would have been just the two of them together in a little pool of electric light. It would have felt intimate and conspiratorial, and, based on past experience and her knowledge of herself, Siobhan thought it quite likely that, after their swim, or even instead of it, they would have had sex. People differ a great deal in this respect, but Siobhan's attitude was very straightforward. Pleasure was a good thing if it didn't hurt anyone, and she was quite open to brief encounters in situations like this where there was little risk of difficult emotional entanglements.

It could have been rather nice actually, she thought a little wistfully, but then she smiled. Sex was such a funny thing when you examined it. She'd always thought that. Such a big deal was made of it. So many contradictory prohibitions and expectations were placed upon it. It was the focal point of so much huffing and blowing and agonising and general nonsense: sonnets, songs, sermons, Viagra, lipstick, rom-coms, operas, jokes, public stonings, pop songs, vows of celibacy, Romeo and Juliet, Ten Top Tips to Wow Your Man in Bed, the pill, the confessional, tears… On and on. So much drama and worry and guilt and longing. And all of it, whether disapproving or celebratory, was centred on sex as a wild and subversive force. Yet what was it in the end? What was that feeling? When you really came down to it, wasn't it just scratching a rather fancy kind of itch? An itch, what's more, that only existed because it ensured that living creatures didn't stint in the business of making more creatures. What was wild about that? What was subversive about a force that pulled all the time, like a kind of biological gravity, in the direction of parenthood and domesticity?

It might start out in the moonlight on a beach, Siobhan thought, but it ended up with stair gates, and car seats, and grown-ups saying 'weewee' and 'poo'.

She had to admit, though, that her thoughts at this point were somewhat coloured by the fact that her friend Anne, back in Dublin, had had a baby a few months ago, and seemed to have lost interest in all the things the two of them had shared. In fact, if it wasn't for that baby, Anne would have been with her now.

And actually, Siobhan thought, in all fairness, and setting jealousy aside, opening your legs and pushing out an entirely new human being who no one had ever seen before, well, that wasn't exactly *tame*. The poo and the stair gates might be, but they were just anodyne trimmings, as Valentine cards and silly pet names were anodyne trimmings for sex. The raw reality was something else.

In fact, when you came to think about, wasn't it life itself that was the really subversive thing? Not just sex but motherhood too? All of life was a rebellion really, a doomed, Lucifer-like rebellion against the peaceful downward pull of entropy, the orderly clock-like unwinding of galaxies and planets and stars.

This last bit, however, came to her more as images than as words, for as sleep took hold, her thoughts ceased to be made of language. They weren't even images really either. They were something more abstract than that: forms, diagram-like chunks of meaning that were as much tactile as visual. Some huge dark falling thing, creatures moving in a moonlit forest, water running downhill in torrents and streams and dripping from sodden peat…

Dear God, she thought, coming awake suddenly, Thomas hadn't even been the first opportunity that day when it came to sex! When she'd asked Spiro about the price of rooms he'd winked and said there was no charge for those who shared his bed. Christ, how sordid! No way was she going to stay there after that! *No* way. Of course the old goat had spotted her distaste almost at once: 'Forgive me my silly joke!' But it didn't fool her. She'd already seen him watching her, eyes slightly narrowed, like a shrewd old fisherman watching his line to see if the bait would be taken. He was about the same age as her dad.

Still, she thought, it had probably worked once, thirty years ago, when Spiro wasn't so flabby and Greece had seemed much more exotic to northern Europeans than it did now in these days when Bali or Thailand were commonplace destinations. The pull of the other. She remembered some nature programme she'd seen. Female chimps sneaking away from their troop when the alpha male was sleeping in his tree, risking attack by leopards to journey all by themselves by moonlight over a mountain ridge and down into the next valley. They'd mate with males from another troop down there and then return again over the rocks and through the leopard-ridden night. Hedging their bets, the programme had said. New genes to mingle with their own.

A leopard in the moonlight. Dear God, imagine that. Those spots among all these speckled shades of grey. The creature would be right on top of you before you'd seen it at all.

Several hours later, she surfaced from sleep again and sat up to have a look around.

The moon had gone, and Orion was right down

at the horizon. This evidence that the planet had been quietly turning while she slept was for some reason immensely comforting, and she felt a surge of that same delicious happiness that had come to her when she found her sleeping bag. It reminded her of when she was a little girl, back in the days before her brothers were even born, wrapped in a warm blanket in the back of her parents' car as they drove through the night to her nan's house in Galway. Sometimes, after an aeon of silence, one of the grown-ups would say something in the front there, some murmured thought or observation, and she'd half-wake to see the street lights of some little town flickering in the windows above her, or maybe the headlights of a passing truck, briefly illuminating the door handles and head-rests, the plastic lining of the car roof, the pocket in front of her, with her pad and crayons, on the back of her father's seat. And then quietness and darkness would return, and she'd slip back down into sleep.

Everything in her immediate surroundings was in almost complete darkness. So was the sea below, except for the faint grey ghosts of waves breaking below her on the beach. There were no fishing boats now, and Thomas had long since gone.

Spring Tide

I remember when I first saw the moon. It was on a summer evening when I was fifteen years old. I was with my two friends, Chaz and Mick, in a disused quarry. The moon was just a couple of nights away from being full, so there was still a sliver of shadow to prove it was a sphere. And when I looked carefully, I could see how the shadow's edge was broken up by the contours of craters.

'Wow, that's amazing,' I said. 'I must have seen the moon hundreds of times but I swear this is the first time I've ever really *seen* it!'

It wasn't just a light in the sky, that's what I was trying to say. It wasn't just a set of facts in some illustrated book about astronomy. It was really there, far away and unreachable perhaps, but every bit as solid an object as I was, and part of the same continuum of space.

'Yeah, nice,' said Chaz. He was busy, and glanced up without any real interest.

'Go on, *look* at it!' I told him. 'It's amazing. The moon's real! It's truly in the world. And so are *we*!'

That last bit was the best part, actually. If the

moon was real and separate from us then we were real too, distinct entities who were also truly in the world. That might seem obvious, but it came to me as a revelation.

You may possibly have guessed by now that we were smoking weed at the time, that famous converter of commonplace observations into amazing insights and half-baked philosophies. In fact, right then, while I was still staring at the moon, my two friends were splitting open a cigarette over an assemblage of Rizla papers, heating an oily hunk of hash, and crumbling it onto the dry brown strands to make our second joint of the evening. Hence their lack of interest in my discovery.

I smoked a considerable amount of weed back then. I didn't think of it as a problem, though in fact I was stealing quite regularly from my parents just to help me fund the habit. Over the next few years, I was to increase my consumption to a point where I lit up as soon as I woke in the morning, and again last thing at night, for the world just seemed too empty, too drained of meaning, without that THC in my veins to bring it alive.

But all the same, acknowledging all of that, I still don't think my insight about seeing the moon was simply the product of being stoned, because that distinction between seeing a thing in the everyday sense and *really* seeing it, does still seem meaningful to me even now, more than forty years on. What's

more, I'm pretty certain it was something I was grop-
ing towards long before I'd ever smoked the stuff.
In fact, I'd go as far as to say that the reason I was so
drawn to the weed in the first place was that I longed
to *see*, and was casting about for ways of doing so.

The funny thing is that Chaz and Mick and I liked
to think of ourselves as rebels, inspired visionaries,
using drugs to smash our way out of the dim half-
world where most people seemed content to live
out their cautious and conformist lives. It only really
strikes me now that we may have had that the wrong
way round. Those who most long to see are not
the visionaries but the ones who can see the least.
Those who long to break free are the ones who are
the most confined. I wonder if some of the famous
artists who are praised for their vision were not so
much experts in seeing, as people who had to work
very hard indeed in order to be able to see anything
at all.

I was a bright kid and, a couple of years later, in spite
of doing very little work, I got myself a place at a
university. It was a disaster. Without the rudimentary structure that had been provided by school, I
stopped working altogether, failed all my first year
exams and duly dropped out. I fell out badly with my
parents over that. They said some cruel things which
I found hard to forget or forgive, specially my bully
of a dad, and I decided to punish them by doing
nothing with my life at all.

I was already with Josie by then. I'd met her at a rock concert in King's Lynn when I was seventeen. (I remember gold-painted Artex walls, smelly toilets, interminable guitar solos.) I had been getting rather panicky about the fact that I'd never had a girlfriend and had no idea how to go about finding one. It was hard enough making friends from among my own gender. Driven by desperation, and fortified by enough cheap cider to make staying upright a fairly challenging task, I attempted to chat up a shy-looking girl who seemed to have come to the gig all on her own. She responded, to my amazement, with enthusiasm.

I decided at once that I was going to fall in love with her and yet, at the same time, on that very same evening in King's Lynn, I experienced doubts. I still remember the questions going through my addled head, queasy with booze, assaulted by prog rock. Had I really made a choice here? What was wrong with this girl anyway, that she should be on her own, and be interested in someone like me? Weren't her ears a bit big, and wasn't there something a bit desperate about her? And wasn't it all a bit repulsive: her desperation, my desperation, those ears? I suppressed those thoughts as soon as I had them – I was seventeen, I'd never had sex, I'd been afraid that sex would always be beyond my reach, and to turn away from Josie then would have been like a starving man turning down a food parcel – but I couldn't expel them altogether. My doubts about her, and about my own motives, were there from the beginning, digging and gnawing away. (Not that I was such a great catch either, of course. Josie's apparent enthusiasm for me presumably also involved suppressing her awareness of certain things, such as my poor personal hygiene, my bad breath, and my utter inability to ask her questions about herself.)

Josie also went to university and, unlike me, managed to stick out the full three years. When she was in her second and third years, I lived with her, sleeping in her room, picking up various temporary jobs in bars and so forth, and otherwise watching daytime TV and smoking weed.

Josie scraped a degree, but she had no idea what to do next, and, as her contemporaries gradually launched themselves out into the world like baby birds taking wing, she and I clung to our now-familiar twig, trying to carry on a student life without either study or fellow students. It was actually quite scary, no matter how much weed we smoked. It was like one of those anxiety dreams in which you've somehow lost the ability to move forward. But Josie finally managed to get herself an administrative post in a hospital in King's Lynn and we both returned to the area we'd grown up in. I went along to a few IT courses, found I was pretty good at picking up this stuff, and in due course stumbled into a temporary job helping to set up a new computer network for the local council in that part of Norfolk, back in the days when PCs were something new.

That job, in its essentials, I still do now. I've taken on a few extra roles and responsibilities over the years, and local government has restructured many times, but I'm still part of the IT team, still based in an office that's less than twenty miles from the small town where I was born, and still basically spend my time sorting out the problems that local government officers have with their PCs. My teachers at school had once expected a good deal more from me, I knew, but this is how I am. I flounder, I grab hold of whatever comes to hand, and then I cling on.

Josie and I stuck together in that exact same way. In the best moments we sort of peacefully co-existed. In the worst, we punished each other, undermined each other, poured cold water on each other's hopes and dreams. If she found something hard that I found easy, I would feel ashamed of her and let her know it. If she did well at something I found hard, I would hate her for showing me up. Our sense of togetherness, such as it was, came mainly from the fact that, when we both found the *same* things hard, both of us together would pour scorn on the things that others could do and we could not: them and their flashy holidays, their fancy jobs, their attractive friends, their seemingly happy relationships.

Deep down we despised ourselves. We hated the fact that there was no love story behind us, just two lonely and unconfident people who'd noticed each other's availability at an utterly forgettable event, and grabbed hold of one another because that seemed preferable, or at least less frightening, than the alternative of remaining alone. And of course we soon had kids to distract us from ourselves, and to give us a reason for being together.

But when the last of our children had left home, there was nothing left for us to hide behind. Rational human beings might have sat down at that point, figured out a way of sharing out their resources, found two new places to live, and parted calmly. It would have been entirely doable for us, at least in a practical sense – we each had a lump sum coming to us at retirement, and a reasonable pension – but that's not what we did at all.

No. We fought. There were scores to be settled, slights to be avenged, and we fought without restraint, screaming out forty years' worth of hate and bitterness and disappointment into one another's faces. Sometimes we flung things or smashed things, and once or twice we even began to hit out at each other, clawing at each other's cheeks, pulling each other's hair. Mostly, though, we just argued and shouted, on and on, until we were sufficiently exhausted to crawl off to sleep for a few hours, or at least lie down and try to sleep, in separate beds as far apart as possible, before resuming battle again the next day. It was horrible, sickening, terrifying, and it went on for several weeks, bizarrely interspersed with ordinary things like work, and walking the dog, and putting out the bins. And still neither of us made the decision to leave.

One Sunday morning we were sitting at our kitchen table, fighting as usual, and Josie had embarked on a long litany of my faults and shortcomings over many years.

'… and you're selfish, Bob. You're selfish and self-righteous and *unbelievably* self-centred. You act like you're the only person in the world with—'

'Oh come on, not all this again. You know I could say exactly the same things about—'

'Excuse me, Bob, I haven't finished. You act like you're the only one with feelings, the only one with legitimate explanations. There's always a perfectly good reason for everything you do wrong. It's always someone else's fault, and nearly always mine. When you shagged that poor silly secretary and broke her heart, it was because I wasn't giving you good enough sex. When you went storming out in a sulk, leaving me to deal with the house and kids, it was because I was creating an atmosphere which you couldn't be expected to tolerate. But *I'm* not allowed an excuse, am I? Every possible explanation I offer for what I do, you dismiss out of hand. In fact, you provide counter-evidence. You quote conversations and precedents from years and decades ago. You cite your so-called friends, who you've discussed me with in detail, and agree with you entirely. You prove beyond all reasonable doubt that you are entirely blameless, entirely virtuous, entirely and tragically misunderstood. You turn everything back onto—'

'What, and you don't do the—?'

Josie's eyes flashed warningly. 'I haven't finished, Bob. You'll get your say when I'm done.'

I shrugged.

'You turn everything back on to me,' Josie persisted. 'I hardly dare to say anything even slightly critical because I know quite well that, even if it's just me asking you if you could empty the dishwasher sometimes, or if you could turn off the tap properly so it doesn't drip, I'll end up getting a two hour lecture.'

And then she stopped, abruptly and, to me, entirely unexpectedly, because her tirade had sounded as if it had enough momentum to continue for some time yet. 'Okay, I'm done,' she said. 'Now it's your turn.'

Well, naturally I'd been preparing my riposte while she was talking. It was to have been constructed in my now-classic three-pronged format. Prong One: what she said about my behaviour was completely untrue. Prong Two: even if it *was* true, it was equally true of her and probably more so. Prong Three: she was to blame for my bad behaviour anyway, because she'd pushed me into a position where I had no choice.

It was all very familiar and well-tried stuff, and I could almost have delivered it in my sleep. But, unusually, I found myself hesitating. I couldn't help noticing, you see, that she'd rather anticipated

Prong Three. And more unusually, I couldn't help feeling she had a point. True, she sometimes did engage in tactics that weren't so very different to mine, but that didn't actually alter the truth of what she said. I *was* self-centred. I was indeed unbelievably self-righteous, 'unbelievably' in a quite literal sense, actually, for even *I* didn't believe in the claims to righteousness which I habitually made. (After all, if I did believe them, why was I always so desperately defensive?) So not only was Prong Three (her being to blame for my faults) a non-starter, but Prong One (me not *having* any faults) wasn't really going to hold water either. And that being so, wasn't Prong Two (her faults being as bad as, or worse than, mine) a little shaky also? Couldn't she quite justifiably claim that some of her own apparent bad behaviour was simply a necessary defence?

I opened my mouth to speak, found I had nothing to say, and closed it again. I still felt angry with her, still felt like the victim of an injustice, but I somehow couldn't find the formula that would clearly establish this to be the case. I stood up and picked up the kettle with the idea of buying time by making another drink. Then I realised that the very idea of one more cup of tea was making me feel sick, and laid it down again unfilled.

'I don't know about you, but I could do with a break. Why don't we take the dog over to the marsh for a couple of hours?'

I was referring to a big saltmarsh, only about six miles from where we lived. It stretches for more than twenty miles along the coast, and is about a mile across at its widest points, with at least another mile of sand stretching out beyond it at low tide. Josie and I and our mongrel Rex had known it all our lives. It's a strange in-between place that's neither land nor sea, where you can see larks next to seagulls, flowering plants alongside crabs, and sheep grazing on the banks of creeks where trilobite-like crustaceans meander through the brackish water, as if still living in the Cambrian age. Behind the marsh is the true land where farms and villages sit among green and partly wooded hills. Beyond it is a wide sandy beach, with the waves and surf you find on other coasts. But the sea is so far out that, when you stand at the very edge of the true land, it's completely out of sight, and there's only marsh in front of you.

We parked our car and walked straight out onto the partly boardwalked track that crossed the marsh to the beach, Rex bounding ahead of us as usual to find things to sniff, eat and piss on. We'd normally have checked the tides, but with all the emotion and turbulence we hadn't given that any thought, and had been striding along obliviously for half a mile before it occurred to us that the tide was coming in very fast, and that it was going to be a particularly high one.

It was Josie who noticed it first. 'The sea's coming in, Bob. Do you think we ought to turn back?'

By this time the beach in the distance was already covered by sea, along with the outer part of the marsh itself. We'd been so stunned and preoccupied by our own little drama that this entire vista, familiar as it was, had barely impinged on us, other than by providing a soothing background to our troubled thoughts, like a poultice on an infected wound. But now, as we belatedly took stock of what was actually happening in the world beyond our skins, we could see the water rushing in through the creeks all round us, sucking and gurgling as it came.

'Christ, yes, and we'd better be quick.' Now I thought about it, I vaguely remembered hearing something about an unusually high tide this weekend. 'Jesus, look at it! It's coming closer just while we watch.'

The tide didn't normally cover the marsh but it happened from time to time, and when it did, the very shallow gradient meant that the sea came in extremely quickly: every vertical inch it rose took it many yards forward horizontally. We called Rex and started back at a jog. By the time we were halfway to the true dry land, the creeks near us were already overflowing. When we finally reached it, we'd been wading for some time through seawater that came well over our knees, holding hands to support one another. Rex had had to swim.

It was actually quite fun, once we knew we weren't going to drown, and the two of us were laughing like kids by the time we stepped out onto the little strip

of grass and shrubs that divided the marsh from the
fields. While Rex shook brackish water all over us,
we pulled off our shoes to empty them, wringing
out our socks and laying them out on a gorse bush
to dry. Then we stood and looked back out at the
expanse of water that now completely covered our
path. It was pretty impressive. Just in the time since
we'd parked our car, almost all of our familiar marsh
had been submerged, with only here or there a dry
patch standing out above it as a sort of low green-
grey island.

And right then, quite suddenly, as I was standing
there and taking all this in, I realised I was seeing
the moon again. I mean I was really *seeing* it in the
way that I'd done in that quarry at fifteen, with my
weed-befuddled friends. It was an overcast day and
the moon itself was completely out of sight, but the
tangible evidence of its presence and scale was right
there in front of us. For it was the moon that had
covered these two miles of sand and marsh by drag-
ging the entire North Sea towards itself. It was the
moon that had forced us to run. It was the moon
that could well have drowned us, if we'd got as far as
the beach before we noticed the tide.

And that was only the beginning of it. For in fact
the moon had formed this entire landscape. This
enormous no man's land between sea and land,
on which all those countless living things out there
depended, only existed at all because of the moon.
All the denizens of the marsh and the beach beyond,

the gulls, the oyster-catchers, the crabs, and all the millions of worms and molluscs and crustaceans that waited in the mud for the tides: they were all creatures of the moon. The very bodies of many of them took the form they did because of the existence of that colossal sphere of rock that passed over them day after day, bringing them new nourishment each time by pulling the ocean upwards and letting it fall.

I turned towards Josie. I was so excited by this notion that I'd quite forgotten our troubles for the moment, and simply wanted to share with her what I'd seen. But poor Josie didn't know that, and I saw her face flinch in anticipation of some new onslaught. We'd become used to moving to and fro between the business of everyday life and our ancient quarrel and she'd simply assumed that our moment of laughter had passed, and that I was starting up the fight all over again.

'Don't look so worried,' I told her. 'I was only going to say something about the tide.'

'Oh, okay. Yes, it's quite something, isn't it, when it comes in like this?'

'Yes, I…' I looked down into her so-familiar face, wary and exhausted, every trace already gone of her recent laughter. I'd been about to tell her about the moon and the marsh and about that time in the quarry when I was fifteen years old, but now something even stranger was happening. I was seeing *Josie*. I was really *seeing* this person – dogged, stoical and wry – who'd been living alongside me now for nearly forty years. As I stood looking down at her, and she up at me, I wondered if I'd ever really seen her before.

'Remember what you said before we came out?' I asked her.

She was *real*, I was thinking! She was separate from me! Yet somehow we were together, both of us in the same world, standing here face to face under the sky.

Josie sighed. 'I know it's your turn to speak now, Bob, and I know some of the things I said were probably unfair, but could you possibly bear to leave it until we get home?'

'No, listen,' I said. I offered my hand to her, and she very tentatively and reluctantly took it, watching my face all the while, as if expecting some kind of trick. 'Listen, dearest,' I told her. 'I don't want to argue now, and I don't need to talk about it. I just wanted you to know that I've thought about what you said, and it wasn't unfair at all. In fact, quite the contrary, everything you said was completely true.'

She held onto my hand, searching my face uncertainly with those wary, weary eyes. And then suddenly she burst into tears.

I put my arms round her at once and, after a moment of holding back, she melted against me, heaving with sobs. I was weeping too. I called her sweetheart, darling, precious, love. I kissed her on the back of her head. And then she lifted her face towards mine and we kissed one another. We kissed again and again, with lips and tongues, smearing the slippery mixture of her tears and mine all over each other's faces.

I suppose some couples might say of such a moment that it was as if all the years had vanished away and they were right back at the beginning. But our beginning had never been like this. There was no point, not one, in all those years since that crappy little rock concert in King's Lynn at which we'd ever been truly together. We'd been like two creeks side by side that had never quite touched. We'd always been waiting for the tide.

Sky

Jeremy Burnet's neighbours were concerned about him, and the woman who phoned the police said she was calling on behalf of them all. They were fairly sure Mr Burnet was in his house – his car was parked in the street and his bike locked in its usual place – but he hadn't been sighted since a Saturday afternoon just under four weeks ago, when some of them had seen him going out in his car and returning with items from a builder's merchant, power tools and such, although there'd been no sign or sound of any work going on in the house either before then or since. Mr Burnet had looked as if he hadn't washed or shaved for weeks. The woman who called the police had tried to greet him – she'd known him a number of years – but he'd just stared right through her as if he didn't know she was there. And he'd always been such a tidy man, too, the sort that didn't like anything out of place, and yet the garden was now completely overgrown, and the living room curtains at the front had been drawn for months, day and night, while the bedroom curtains were never closed at all.

What had finally prompted this call, though, was that one of the other neighbours had been contacted by Mr Burnet's elderly mother who was too frail to visit him for herself. She said she was worried because her son never phoned any more, and never picked up when she tried to call him. And surely, said the neighbour who'd rung the police, even if Mr Burnet had somehow managed to slip away without any of them noticing, he'd have let his own mother know where he was going?

Two police officers went to Jeremy Burnet's house, a policewoman and a policeman. Their names were Cheryl and Pradeep. They rang the doorbell for several minutes, and then called through the letterbox. 'Hello, Mr Burnet? Are you there? It's the police. Could we have a word? You're not in trouble of any kind, but we're just checking everything's alright. Your neighbours are worried for you.'

There was no answer, though, not even that indefinable feeling of *presence*, that sense of something listening deep inside the house, that in Cheryl's experience you tended to get when someone was in but didn't want to be intruded upon. 'Either he's not there or he's not well at all,' she decided. Pradeep nodded. He was the younger of the two by some years, and tended to defer to his colleague's wider experience.

Cheryl was about to make a call to the station about a warrant to break down the door, when one of the watching neighbours remembered he had a key. Jeremy had given it to him one hot summer several years ago, he said, 'before all of this started', so he could come in and water Mr Burnet's patio plants for him when he was taking a holiday in Spain with his then-girlfriend. Mr Burnet had asked the neighbour to keep it in case he ever locked himself out.

The key turned in the lock, and the two police officers entered, stepping over a drift of mail. The door of the living room was open. There was a cream-coloured sofa and chairs, and expensive-looking curtains drawn across the window. The light was switched on, though it was the middle of the day. However, what they immediately noticed was the wide-open hatch in the middle of the floor, from which a rug had been rolled back and shoved aside. There was a concrete staircase descending inside it, and light shining up from below. It was a very odd place to put a set of cellar stairs, but there they were, and it seemed exceedingly probable that they would find Mr Burnet at the bottom of them.

Cheryl leaned over the hatch and called down the staircase. 'Mr Burnet? Are you down there?'

'We're just checking to see if you're okay,' added Pradeep.

There was no answer, no sense of presence at all, though the echo was surprisingly deep and strong.

Cheryl drew in breath. She had dealt with a few corpses in her time – self-hangings, traffic accidents, a knifing once, a couple of people who'd jumped in front of trains – but you never really grew out of that initial shock of stark primitive horror. 'Okay, Prad. Let's go down and have a look.'

They'd assumed they'd descend for the equivalent of one storey, and perhaps find two damp low-ceilinged rooms down there. But that wasn't what happened. A storey down, the stairs just turned and carried on their descent. The same thing happened again at the next level. It wasn't until the third storey, when there was enough space between them and the living room above to insert another whole house, that everything suddenly opened up. Long corridors, well lit by office strip-lights, radiated out in four directions, with doors and the openings of side corridors arrayed on either side. And the staircase continued on down.

They could feel goosebumps rising on their skin, and a strange, pure, abstract kind of terror.

'Jesus Christ,' muttered Cheryl. 'What *is* this?'

'We need to call for help,' said Pradeep in the particular, slightly strangled, voice he used on the rare occasions he asserted his recent training over Cheryl's considerable experience. He would have been hard-pressed to say what they needed help *with*. Corridors, rooms, stairs: where was the threat in that? Yet Cheryl concurred at once, as almost anyone surely would have done in the same position. The police exist to maintain order, after all, to enforce boundaries. What the two of them had discovered was quite clearly so strange and inexplicable that reinforcements were needed to keep a solid boundary in place between reality and hallucination. Two people were simply not sufficient to reassure one another that what they were seeing was actually there.

'I'll do it,' Cheryl said. There was no signal down there, so she climbed up the stairs again to Mr Burnet's living room and stepped out of the front door to make the call. It was good to see the daylight and hear the sound of traffic on the main road nearby.

Four neighbours were standing out there now. Several more were watching from their own front gates up and down the street. They all searched Cheryl's face for clues.

'Is he…?'

'We haven't found him yet. Do all these houses have cellars?'

'Cellars, no. We don't have a cellar.'

'Us neither. I don't think anyone has one on this street. I've never heard of one.'

Soon two whole van-loads of police arrived, along with an ambulance, while a second patrol car brought a uniformed inspector to take charge. Blue lights flashed importantly and Mr Burnet's house was quickly separated from the everyday world by a magical strip of blue and white tape. Yet what was the emergency? A missing man, and a cellar of implausible magnitude!

A small crowd was beginning to form. Passers-by from the main road at the end of the street saw that something was going on and came wandering up, with a slightly furtive air, to find out more. Several police officers remained outside the house to enforce that stripy blue boundary, while the inspector, a sergeant, a dozen other police officers and two paramedics accompanied Cheryl back into Mr Burnet's living room, and down those strange concrete stairs.

'I had a quick look further down,' Pradeep told them when they joined him in a well-lit corridor, three flights of stairs below the surface. 'Two storeys down actually. It's exactly the same as this on the next two levels – doors, corridors, lights – and the staircase carries on down even after that. I don't know what's going on here, but—'

'*Mr Burnet?*' the inspector interrupted him, cupping his hands round his mouth. 'Mr Burnet? It's the police! Are you alright?' There was a long deep echo and then a silence, which all of them felt a vague need to cover up with activity and talk.

'It must have been here a long time, or people would—'

'I thought I'd seen some pretty weird things in my time, but—'

'Let's try some of these rooms,' the inspector said.

Several officers began opening doors in the corridors. Most of the rooms were completely empty, their white walls and grey lino as pristine as if they had yet to be used. One had a bucket and a mop inside it, another an empty water bottle. Oddly, each door had a blank yellow post-it note stuck to it.

Cheryl glanced at Pradeep. 'Inspector, why don't myself and Pradeep find out just how far down the stairs go?'

The inspector shrugged. Of course he had no more idea of what they were dealing with than anyone else. One of his staff back at the station had made a call to the MOD to ask if this was a nuclear bunker or some such, unlikely as that seemed; others had called the city's planning department, the land registry and a well-known local historian, but no one knew anything about it. There was no record of Mr Burnet's house having any kind of cellar at all, and it had stood there since 1923.

'Sure, why not,' the inspector said. 'Go down to the bottom and report back. If you see anything that worries you on the way, just come straight back up. Meanwhile we'll begin a room by room search of each level from the top down.'

Cheryl and Pradeep counted twenty-two storeys before they finally reached a floor where there were no more stairs going down. Well-lit corridors radiated out from the staircase as they'd done on all of the other twenty-one floors.

'Okay,' Cheryl said, 'so this—'

'Cheryl, look!' Pradeep interrupted.

A couple of metres into one of the corridors, the lino had been torn back and there was a hole with lumps and crumbs of rubble scattered around it.

Feeling very isolated suddenly, very aware that all their colleagues were twenty-one storeys above them, and that all the levels in between were silent and empty, the two police officers crept towards the hole and peered down. It had been roughly cut through over a metre of rock or concrete. There was an aluminium ladder propped up in it, fully extended to a length of about four metres, and its feet were standing in another corridor below them, which looked just like the one they were in.

'Sweet Jesus,' murmured Cheryl.

'I'll call the inspector, right?'

'You won't get a signal.'

'We'd better go up and tell him, then, yeah?'

'Up twenty-one flights of stairs? For him to ask us what's down the ladder, and why didn't we look? Wouldn't it be better to check it out first? Mr Burnet's down there, I'm sure of it.'

Pradeep nodded. He leant over the hole. 'Mr Burnet? It's the police. We're just here to see if you're alright.'

All around them, above, below and on every side, huge empty spaces devoured the sound of Pradeep's human voice – small, sentient, anxious – and turned it back into something pure and inanimate and eternal, like the boom of wind in a deserted canyon, or the echo of a rockfall on Mars.

'Come on,' said Cheryl. 'Let's get this over with. I don't like ladders.'

·

There were more stairs again down there. They descended another twenty-two storeys, with the same four corridors radiating out from the staircase on each level. Down at the bottom, they found another roll of ripped lino, another hole with a ladder in it, and another corridor beneath. It was as if a row of office blocks had been plucked up from the centre of a city and buried, not side by side, but in a stack, one above the other.

'Right,' said Pradeep firmly. 'So *now* we get the inspector.'

'If you want to climb forty-four storeys,' said Cheryl, 'be my guest, Prad. But surely it's obvious that Mr Burnet is still somewhere below us?'

They found him at the bottom of the third block, almost seventy storeys below the surface. He'd been at work on another hole – it was nearly half a metre deep – and his pneumatic drill lay nearby, along with a diesel generator and an empty fuel can. Burnet himself was slumped against a wall, bearded and emaciated, his clothes filthy, his lips dry and cracked.

Cheryl squatted beside him to feel his pulse. 'Mr Burnet? Jeremy?'

His eyes flickered briefly and closed again. One of his hands moved slightly. He was alive, but whether he was conscious or not was hard to tell. When Cheryl took his hand, the fingers seemed to make some effort to close over hers, but perhaps that was just a reflex.

'I'll stay with him,' she said. 'You get up there. We'll need water – he's very dehydrated – and some way of getting him safely up through the holes. Take it steady on those stairs, though, Prad. Sixty-six floors is a lot to climb, even at your age.'

As Pradeep began the ascent, she turned back to Jeremy Burnet. Why had he tried to keep this place a secret? Surely it would be obvious to anyone, as it had been to her and Pradeep, that just the business of being here at all was a task that required a whole team?

'What were you thinking of, Jeremy? Why didn't you tell anyone? No one should keep a thing like this to themselves.'

She glanced at the hole he'd been making when he finally collapsed.

'Yes,' she said. 'And what on earth were you looking for down here? What did you hope to find?'

Thirty or forty onlookers stood out in the street now, beyond the blue and white tape. Several more patrol cars had arrived with lights flashing, along with an outside broadcast van from a local TV station.

A hush descended as the paramedics emerged with the stretcher. Revived somewhat by water and glucose, Jeremy couldn't move his head much because he'd been tightly strapped in to keep him safe while he was being manoeuvred through the holes and up the stairs, but he could hear the people out there murmuring to one another, and the crackling voices from the police radios, and the traffic passing on the main road nearby. He raised a tentative hand in greeting and, to his surprise, there was a cheer from the crowd in response.

Cheryl bent over him briefly as the paramedics lifted the stretcher into the ambulance, checking that he knew where he was and what was happening. Her face was kind but puzzled. Hundreds of metres above her, long white clouds, tinged with grey, were blowing by. Two crows were flying beneath them, calling out to one another from time to time as they crossed that immense vault beneath the sky.